EVALUATING THE ELF

MONSTER MAGIC DATING SERVICE
BOOK FIVE

L.A. BORUFF DAPHNE MOORE
USA TODAY BESTSELLING AUTHORS

Book Design by L.A. Boruff

1

CASSIE

I NORMALLY LOVED GOING to the beach. This time was an exception, mostly because I'd never wanted to be an extra in a real-life version of that Hitchcock bird movie.

The car door slammed behind me, and I bolted across the dunes, my hair flapping behind me in the salty breeze. My foot slipped out of a sandal, but I didn't stop to retrieve it, skip-hopping toward the center of the disturbance.

The beach was in havoc, a whirlwind of feathers and screeches, people running for cover, and a few stupidheads standing around with their phones out gawking.

"Damn it." The soft sand was gritty and damp against my bare foot. There was no time to worry about a lost shoe when the sky above was thick with gulls. They were everywhere, like a storm cloud of wings and beaks, their cries piercing the air.

I charged at the center of the storm, where a song threaded through the calamity. Pure, ethereal, haunting. The singer was, of course, an elf. Because I really needed this today.

More birds arrived in response to the siren call of her voice.

The elf stood at the top of an artful pile of rocks, both arms stretched upwards toward the squawking mass, her pale skin almost glowing against the darkening sky.

"Beautiful, just wonderful," I grumbled.

A handful of men and women, too entranced or too stupid to seek cover, gawked at her. Their attention was totally fixed on the elf, whose slender form was barely concealed by what looked like layers of sheer fabric, clinging to her curves and fluttering in the wind. The material was damp from the sea spray, adding to the effect.

Of course, she also looked like a CGI team had enhanced her. All she needed was a soundtrack.

"Hey." I tried to shout over the noise, but my voice didn't carry far enough. I had to get closer.

I felt it before I saw it. A wet splat hit my shoulder, followed by another plop on my head.

"Ugh, gross." My temper flared hot and quick as I swiped my hair back, not daring to look down at what I knew would be a smeared mess on my shirt. The world was literally crapping on me, and I'd had enough.

"Stop singing!" I yelled, finally close enough to the elf to be heard over the winged frenzy. She turned in slow motion, long dark hair somehow both damp and flowing, and faced me, a faint smirk playing on her lips.

"Stop? Why?" The elf's reply was song, each word a note that seemed to dance on the salty air. Her face sparkled with mischief.

"Because people could get hurt." My patience was wearing thin. My voice was mundane compared to hers, but at this point, I didn't care. I was *done* with elf mischief.

"Look at them." I pointed toward a group of people huddled under a small shelter, their faces masks of fear as gulls swooped dangerously close, their beaks sharp and menacing.

I ignored the people in plain sight. Presumably if they were pecked, they'd run for cover too.

My jaw clenched as the elf shook her head, her expression shifting to stubborn refusal. "No," she said, "it's time for the gulls to get even for all the human cruelties."

"Are you kidding me?" Anger surged through my veins, hot and potent. "Have you no brains? They'd probably be happy with some fish being left out or something, not pecking people's eyes out." My voice rose, its timbre laced with an authority I didn't fully understand but could feel pulsing at my core.

The elf tilted her head, considering me as if I were

a curious specimen rather than a threat. Her indifference poured fuel on my mad.

"Stop this." The words erupted from me. They rippled out through the air, resonating deeper than I'd intended.

Something inside me clicked into place, the power in me I'd discovered a little while ago. It was hard to get it to work, but in response to my anger, the invisible force reached out toward the elf, compelling her to heed my words.

She blinked, taken aback, her song faltering. "Very well," she said with a graceful flick of her long fingers. With a flutter of translucent draperies, she turned on her heel and flounced off, leaving no tracks on the damp sand.

As the magic in her melody dissipated, the frenzied circling and swooping of the birds slowed, their calls dying down rather than almost deafening me. Half the gulls landed near discarded food, pecking at it, happy to fill their bellies when not driven by the elf's desire. The air was suddenly filled with human voices, an annoyed chorus replacing the deadly melody.

"Tell Aiden we need to talk!" I yelled after her, my voice slicing through the angry commentary of the people emerging from their shelters. The elf, a mere wisp of translucence against the chaotic backdrop, didn't turn back but raised a hand in vague acknowledgment. Or was it dismissal? Either way, the message should get through.

I marched off the beach, one shoe missing, the wet sand squelching between my toes. Ignoring the mess on my shoulder, I trudged back to my car.

Mission accomplished. Whee.

"Hey, you there. Can I get a quick word about what just happened?" A young guy with a phone in hand approached me, the unmistakable eagerness of a stringer on his face.

"Look, if you want an interview about the elves, call Repupair." I brushed past him. "Andromeda Quinn is their representative. Otherwise, no comment."

"Got it." He snapped a photo before I could protest. "Your name is?"

"Cassie." I bared my teeth at him in a maybe smile. "Hope you have a great day."

"Thanks, Cassie. This will make an interesting piece," he said after me, already tapping away on his phone.

"Sure, as long as it doesn't come back to bite me," I said under my breath, thinking how my sister Roma, would have to work to spin this one. Franklin's absence had left a void, but together, she was great at keeping the PR ship afloat and headed in the right direction.

Now, if only those damned birds would disperse.

I SLAMMED the door of my apartment behind me, my emotion from the day finally boiling over. My shirt was a disaster, the bird poop dried a second skin in the time it took to get home after three different accidents snarled traffic even worse than usual.

My hair felt like it had been styled with tar. I didn't bother glancing at the mirror in the entryway. I didn't need to confirm how terrible I must look.

"Shower," I said to myself as if I needed the reminder. Stripping off my ruined shirt, I tossed it into the hamper with more force than necessary. It would be a nice challenge for the dry cleaners later, but right now, I couldn't care less.

The hot water from the shower head was a miracle, finally able to wash away the physical reminders of my no good very bad day. As I lathered my hair, gritty with salt, sand and bird poop, I tried to focus on something other than memory. The clean herbal scent of the shampoo, water cascading all around me, anything other than that song and splat.

"Cassie, deal with it." I tried to drown out the mental noise. The elf's song lingered in my ears, an eerie melody. That was how all elfsong was, a horrible earworm.

"Stop it." I shook my head to dispel the memory. Steam enveloped me, the mirror fogging up, I focused on the now, the scalding spray, the quiet. Just me in the shower, reclaiming my space, my peace.

When I finally shut off the water, stepping out onto the fuzzy green bathmat, I felt looser, less frazzled. The disorder of the beach receded from me, now my sister's problem.

My problem was unless I concentrated on not thinking about my responsibilities, the need to mediate between this world and the elves, they came right back into my face.

"Tomorrow's problem," I told my reflection, now just a vague outline in the misted-over mirror. "Tonight, you relax."

Wrapped in a towel with another twisted up in my hair, I plopped down onto the suede couch. The fabric felt cool against my skin, a contrast to the day's heat and the lingering warmth from my shower. I let out a long sigh that seemed to carry every fire I'd put out today.

I leaned back, trying to keep myself relaxed. My disobedient mind raced, replaying the day's events. The elf, her song and words, the racket of the gulls. It would have been so nice if they'd stayed a myth, a fairy tale, not mayhem generators coming to my local beach.

"Dammit, Aiden," I said under my breath, wondering when the Elf King's son would deign to appear. He'd made the deal with me back in Dream. In exchange for innocent humans being released back to Earth, the elves could once again visit earth under my supervision.

I'd thought that he would control them as well. Silly me. Here I was, chasing after his kin like some glorified nanny. I never signed up to babysit a bunch of sociopathic hyperactive adult toddlers.

My phone buzzed on the coffee table, its screen lighting up with a message. Work, probably. Probably Roma, knee-deep in PR crises thanks to the elves' latest stunt.

On the other hand, Roma's wedding with the Goblin King could help me corral the elves. There was no way they'd miss that event.

And I'd have help from the other kings in keeping the elves out of trouble, since they liked Bran and would want his wedding trouble free.

I reached for the phone again, this time with purpose. Tapping swiftly, I composed a new message and hit send, watching as it appeared in our group chat.

Roma needs to marry on Fellmere Island, right? Any date yet?

The screen lit up almost immediately.

Shay: Island venue, yes. My head's too full to deal with wedding plans right now." 😵🥴

Roma: I could do small. Way too swamped with monster PR to think about a big event.

Heh. No, big sister, it's going to be a big wedding for you. Before I typed my reply, Tanni's message stopped the conversation, her tone firm even in text form.

Tanni: It has to be grand, Roma. Bran is royalty, and we need the positive press. Think of the optics.

I sighed, dislodging my towel as I ran a hand through my still-damp hair. Tanni had a point. A royal wedding would play well for everyone involved.

Roma: Fine.

I grinned as I tapped on my phone.

A big blowout it is.

The messages kept coming, a stream of pings and vibrations. Lots of ideas and suggestions, as irresistible as the incoming tide. I made my decision when Tanni started sending bullet-pointed lists of what needed to be done and when.

Tanni: Look, we all have a lot going on.

I typed back, my thumbs moving with practiced ease.

I'll take care of the wedding details. Stop worrying.

Roma: Are you sure?

The undercurrent of relief was palpable even through the cold digital text.

Roma: You're a lifesaver, Cassie.

Sure as I'll ever be.

My gut flipped at the memory of my wedding.

Well, the planning wasn't what messed that marriage up.

Roma: Thanks so much! 🩶💕

Shay sent a separate message to me only.

Shay: Remember, it has to be on the island.

Shay: It's the only safe place for her.

I paused, the words sinking in.

I know.

I kept it short. Shay's visions were almost never wrong, and that one, Roma dying if she married anywhere but the island, was a frightening weight to carry.

Tanni: Cassie is the best!

It sounded more like a cheer than part of a chat.

I locked the phone and tossed it onto the couch beside me, leaning back and closing my eyes.

The island venue made things complicated, true, but nothing I couldn't handle. The responsibility of orchestrating a spectacle worthy of royalty rested on my shoulders. I could do this.

"Just have to figure out how to get the elves to calm the heck down," I said into the silence of the room. "That's going to be so easy. Not."

2
AIDEN

I SWUNG my leg over the saddle and dismounted, letting my horse's reins hand free. He moved over to munch on the blossoms of the apple tree next to us. That tree never stopped blooming, and the petals had a pleasant, honeyed taste that we both enjoyed.

The view from the mountainside was breathtaking as any other prospect in Alfheim. Unformed magic tinged the crisp mountain air, though this area had deeper roots in reality thanks to our recent human guests.

Even here, the enemy, boredom, clamped my mind. Though lovely, the view became tiresome; the rolling green of the forest cascading down below me like an emerald river, commonplace. Cu, my horse, cantered down the side of the mountain, seeking a fogbank to rest in while I thought.

"Dull," I said under my breath. I didn't will the landscape to shift, since everyone benefited from reality rooting in Alfheim. My over responsibility was why all my compatriots viewed me as a total bore.

The land's perfection held no interest without flaws. Humans yearned for the flawless, elves had learned the boredom of perfection too well.

We enjoyed the Earth for its charming blend of beauty and ugliness.

When traveling, the dimension Dream when it slept was entertaining; part of the fun being tweaking Martellus the Troll King. Bran, the Goblin king was the titular king of Dream, but Martellus was Dream's own child and had more say in whether or not Dream permitted change.

Also, he was stodgy and easily exasperated, always good for a laugh.

I called for my fiddle mentally and turned to find it nestled against the base of an ancient pine. Body under my chin and bow in my hand, the strings vibrated with life when I drew the bow across them. A melody filled the air, weaving between the trees. It carried my thoughts forward, away from the stillness of my location.

What to do next? The tune circled that question, spiraling toward an answer that eluded me. I needed something... other. My bow moved faster, the song growing wilder, chasing the pulse of adventure that thrummed just out of reach.

The last note of my fiddle's song faded into silence as I pondered recent events. The barrier to the human world had been lowered after I bargained with a human, Cassandra. Cassie Quinn, she called herself. With those barriers gone, a fresh influx of humans had come into Alfheim.

Since the Formless Ones, our ancient enemies and cousins already had a foothold on that world, it was best to preserve some of the inhabitants. While we elves had a bad reputation, we didn't strip and destroy worlds before moving on. The Formless Ones did.

There was always someone stupid and greedy enough to let them in.

"Or we could war." The idea left a bitter taste. We shared ancestry with the Formless Ones, yet our choices had diverged long ago. They chose possession and ruin, while we elves enjoyed the tangible, the richness of life embodied. Their incursions spelled disaster for worlds, though to be honest our revels could be destructive as well.

In the past, when we both found a world we coveted, we fought. That left behind scorched realities, all mortal life caught between us ended by an ancient feud.

In the beginning of those conflicts, we offered sanctuary, sometimes called captivity, to a chosen few. A conservation effort of sorts, preserving pieces of what was lost within the malleable bounds of Alfheim. Their worlds could be recreated by them, making the loss less.

It was a heavy thought, one that weighed on me even as I tucked my fiddle away.

An image of Cassie flashed through my mind. She was an enigma, a human brimming with untapped magical potential. Her power simmered beneath the surface, raw and untrained, like a nearly irresistible perfume for me. Also, a beacon for the Formless Ones.

A prize either way.

"Blast," I swore softly, feeling the stirrings of concern. When they sensed her, they would try to possess her. As I'd seen her, Cassie was vulnerable, her defenses untested. Yet a fire burned in her that couldn't be ignored. That flame could save her or doom her, depending on how the winds of fate and luck blew.

Intervention was called for, and I was the man to do it.

The crunch of gravel underfoot drew my attention away from my now more pleasant thoughts. I turned to see a tall, thin woman making her way up the mountain path with an ease that made the sleep climb look easy. Her gray hair caught the light of Alfheim's eternal dawn, and her slight smile held secrets as deep as the valley she had traversed.

"Hello, Luck," I greeted her as she approached, dismissing the concept of coincidence. She had a knack for appearing precisely when least expected but most needed. Or when you wanted her least.

With a slight tilt of her head, the smile playing around the corners of her mouth deepening, she corrected me. "I go by Ms. Fortuna now, thank you." Her voice was smooth, like the fine silk tunics favored by the high elves of the eastern glades.

"Ms. Fortuna." I tipped an imaginary hat her way. "What brings you to this mountain, this day?"

"Your interest in the human Cassie." She folded her hands neatly, "has not gone unnoticed by me."

"Do you plan to intervene?" I asked, keeping my tone light.

"Not at all, but her fortune is about to shift." Ms. Fortuna's attention felt heavy as a stone on my back, her words landing even before she spoke them. "Cassie's ex-husband has made a dark bargain with the Formless Ones. He plans to trade her to them, shift the possession from him to her."

My fingers tightened around my fiddle. "That spineless worm," I said. Cassie, for all her raw, untrained magic and fiery spirit, wouldn't stand a chance without aid.

I stood up abruptly, casing fiddle and bow. "Not on my watch," I said. Cassie had reached out to me via another elf earlier, something about wanting to meet up, and I'd been too distracted to respond. Now, it seemed like fate had nudged me.

"Thank you for the heads up, Luck," I said, not bothering with her preferred name. She simply nodded, an enigmatic smile still playing on her lips.

Knowing what would probably happen and not telling anyone much was one of her most annoying quirks.

With a sharp whistle, I called for Cu. He materialized from the mists that clung to the mountain's flank, his ethereal form solidifying into muscle and sinew as he ran up the mountain to my side. Mounting in one fluid motion, I nudged the beast forward into the air, willing us to cross the veil.

The transition between worlds was always a jolt, the first crossing calling a rush of magic that pricked at the skin like a thousand tiny needles. Once attuned to your destinations, the sensation became more bearable, tingles rather than sharp jabs.

I opted to pass through Dream first. The veil parted around me and my steed, like curtains drawn back by an unseen hand.

Within the realm of Dream, I needed to tread carefully; Dream had awakened and held its secrets close. It also seemed to have some quarrel with my father or grandfather; I'd never inquired as to the details. Dream had slept since my earliest childhood and had been an interesting place to visit. Now it woke, and the dangerous edge it took made it an even more interesting place.

"By the pact sealed by Cassie's word, I take passage." I focused on the delicate threads of the contract she had unwittingly woven when she bargained with me. The barrier shivered, then softened, allowing me entry to Earth.

"Now we see if we can turn Luck on her ear," I said to Cu as we emerged in the air over the city Cassie called home. He descended to the street, and I dismounted.

The city's pulse thrummed beneath our feet, a roar of human life that felt foreign after the ethereal silence of Alfheim.

So many people, so many merchants lining the streets behind walls of glass. All different sorts of shops, all gathered to attract attention to their wares.

Across the street, a pet store. That one's wall of glass was alive with the movement of small creatures pacing in their confined spaces.

With a flicker of dislike, I stepped off the curb. My horse's equine form melted away to be replaced by a lean, silver-furred dog. People passed us without a second glance, accepting the loyal pet that now walked beside me.

We entered the pet store, a bell tinkling above the door announcing our arrival. Rows upon rows of cages lined the walls, each a small prison containing a feathered or furred inhabitant. The air was heavy with a mix of scents: sawdust, kibble, and an underlying hint of desperation.

"Can't say I like this sort of shop," I said, attention lingering on a parrot preening itself with half-hearted pecks. "You lot should have a voice to tell these folks how you're feeling."

My companion, now in dog form, whined softly, pressing against my leg. A silent understanding passed between us. We both knew the natural world didn't abide by such rules, but that didn't mean we had to like it.

I raised my hand, fingers weaving through the air as I whispered an incantation. Magic pulsed from my palm, invisible threads stretching out to touch each animal within the store. A hum of energy buzzed, and then silence fell, broken abruptly by a chorus of words.

"Excuse me," came a haughty, slightly nasal voice, "my water is tepid and tastes like plastic." Startled, I turned to see a fluffy Persian kitten, its blue eyes fixed on a young employee who stood frozen, a water jug in hand.

"Also," the kitten said, unabashed, "the kibble's stale. It offends my palate. Do better."

The employee blinked, his mouth opening and closing like a fish out of water. Around us, other animals joined in with their own complaints and demands, creating a cacophony of critter commentary.

Satisfied, I gave a nod of approval. It wasn't every day I could correct a wrong, however small. With a last glance at the emancipated animals around me, I beckoned Cu with a jerk of my head. "Let's go."

We left the pet store behind, the newly vocal inhabitants still making their opinions known. Fresh air hit my face, and I smiled, reveling in the minor anarchy I'd left in my wake. It was time to find Cassie. Her home was not far from here.

I strode down the bustling street, Cu trotting at my side, the clamor of modern city life enveloping us. The way people bustled about, consumed by who knew what, made it a peculiar yet amusing place.

My mind moved elsewhere, to Cassie.

She intrigued me. I had seen her wield her latent power with an innocent clumsiness. Beneath her controlled exterior, her magic seethed like a tempest contained in human form, wild, untamed, and utterly captivating. Then there was her outward appearance: she possessed curves and an earthy grace lacking in the women of my people, a warm contrast to the often-chosen forms of elven women.

I admired the way she moved, all grace and fire rolled into one.

Boredom vanished as I remembered how she'd flare up when riled, her cheeks blossoming into shades of crimson while she launched into a tirade. It was quite the spectacle. Cassie didn't just get angry; she became the embodiment of fury itself, something to behold and never forget.

As quickly as the joy came, it faded. A shadow came to my thoughts, that her vibrancy was as ephemeral as a human lifespan. Cassie would age, wither, and pass from this world as all mortals must.

That, I admitted to myself, would be a great sorrow.

Unless I made a bargain with her, to grant her the elixir, an expensive and time-consuming concoction that would extend her life. But I needed to bargain with her for it, and first she had to know about it and want it. I'd need to work on that,

"Come on," I urged Cu, my new project in mind. "We have someone very special to see."

3
CASSIE

I SPRAWLED ON THE COUCH, half a dozen pillows jammed under my back. Still wearing my comfy cotton pajamas, covered in kittens chasing butterflies, I had my laptop balanced precariously on my knees.

The screen glowed with a dozen open tabs, each one a rabbit hole leading deeper into the labyrinth of wedding planning. Each contained information on providers from florists to photographers. My job was comparing the prices and styles. To do it right, planning a wedding required meticulousness that bordered on obsessiveness.

"Outdoor or indoor? Buffet or plated? How many

entree options?" I said into the notes app on my phone. "Classical quartet or DJ?"

The question transported me back to another time, another set of decisions. I'd thought they led to my happily ever after. The image of Franklin, my ex-husband, flashed across my mind.

Acid climbed out of my stomach.

"Damn it," I hissed, slamming the laptop shut. The anger surged like a tidal wave, threatening to drag me under. The memory of him, standing at the altar, making promises he hadn't planned to keep, clawed at my insides.

I inhaled slowly, forcing the hot tide of rage back into its mental box. This wasn't about me. Opening the laptop again, I refused to let the ghost of betrayal derail me.

Focus, Cassie. "This will be the best wedding ever. I have a goal." Imagining her reaction if I went overboard soothed my raw nerves. Shay had offered to help defray the costs. Bran had told me to spend as I wished. I could make this the wedding to top. The room was silent except for my chuckle. Oh, this could be fun.

Scrolling through caterers' websites, I paused at each menu, trying to imagine what would please an audience far from ordinary. "Exotic fruit for the vampires, obviously." I made a note on a sticky pad. Tanni had told me that they very much enjoyed fruits. "Something raw for the shifters... What kind of tartare would be best?"

I clicked on a site with an array of exotic dishes, wondering what if any dietary restrictions trolls had. From what little comment Shay made, I'd gotten the impression Martellus' people enjoyed strong flavors. One dish boasted a spicy inferno sauce that seemed interesting visually and in its taste.

"That might just work," I said, picturing the flames. Would they find it kitschy or perfect? I added it to the list anyway; this was a brain-storming session.

"Let's see, for the fae folk... go the ironic route and serve them something light and ethereal?" I drummed my fingers on the table, thinking. "A salad with edible flowers, maybe some honey vinai-grette?" That sounded right. They were all hunting and meat.

"So many different peoples." I shook my head. Who knew planning a menu for such a diverse crowd would be like navigating a culinary minefield? But I'd make it happen. I could do this.

The chime of the doorbell snapped me out of my focus. I glanced at the clock; it was only midmorning. Shuffling to the door in my pajamas, I peeked at the security camera feed. Aiden stood on my doorstep, his silver-blonde hair like a halo in the sunlight, a faint smile on his lips.

I opened the door, ready to send him on his way. Wait, I'd said I wanted to talk to the elf earlier. Him coming so fast probably meant trouble somewhere.

"Good morning, Cassie," he greeted, his low voice smooth as silk.

"Morning," I said curtly, crossing my arms. "Is there trouble?"

"I'm answering your request to talk. I believe I have a solution to some of our problems. Your role as a liaison isn't official." Aiden stepped into my living space uninvited. "You must stand before the king with me and have him affirm it. The current agreement is solely between us."

"Great, more red tape. Anything else?" I asked, my tone sharp. I didn't like the fact that I found him attractive.

"Elven customs dictate that for any service requested, a bargain must be struck. We do not offer aid without reciprocation." He held my gaze, his own aloof but somehow challenging.

"Is that so? What exactly will you get out of helping me chase down your unruly elves?" I asked, irritation flaring.

"Amusement," he said simply, lips curling at the edges.

"Good to know." I controlled the urge to tap my fingers impatiently against my leg. A question about the upcoming wedding occurred to me. "For future reference, does that cover gifts? Do those come with strings attached too?"

"Gifts are objects given freely, not services. They are separate matters entirely," Aiden said, a hint of condescension lacing his words.

"Right. When do we leave to see the king to make this whole thing official?" I asked.

"As soon as you are ready." Aiden spread his fingers in the direction of my pajamas. "You might want to prepare yourself for the journey."

"Give me a minute," I said, annoyance and curiosity flickering within me. It would be a good break from the endless tabs of wedding plans, freshening my mind.

Changing quickly into sturdy chinos and a scoop neck red top, I pulled my hiking boots out of the closet and laced them on. Grabbing the bag that matched the top, I was back out in the living room in record time. I dropped my phone and wallet into the bag and then raised an eyebrow in Aiden's direction.

Aidan extended his hand toward me. For the flicker of my hesitation, I studied his face, the sharpness of his jawline, the intensity of his blue eyes, and something else... a friendly warmth I hadn't expected from him. So, I took his hand.

Instantly, tingle spread through my fingers, up my arm, and enveloped my entire being. I glanced down in awe as my bronze skin shimmered with a thousand tiny lights, like I was dusted with stars. “What’s this?"

"Magic," Aidan said calmly. "It will protect you as we pass through Dream to Alfheim."

"Feels... nice," I said reluctantly, not wanting to know I didn’t know much on this topic.

"Watch closely now," he said, and his gaze lifted to focus on something I couldn't see. The air before us began to swirl, an intricate dance of colors that mesmerized me. It twisted and turned, forming a vortex that reminded me of what an unsecured silk scarf did on my shoulders when caught in a gust of wind.

Then the colors parted.

Through the veil, a thick mist greeted us, rolling and shifting as if alive. We stepped forward together, and the mist clung to my skin, cool and damp. When it finally cleared, a dense forest loomed around us, trees reaching high into glimpses of a sky that seemed both foreign and familiar.

"Is this Alfheim?" I asked, looking around.

"Yes," Aidan said. "Welcome to my world."

I stepped forward, details of the forest materializing around me as if painted by an invisible brush. The tree's leaves formed a mosaic of vivid greens that seemed too vibrant to be real. Moss carpeted the ground, and somewhere in the distance, a brook babbled its secrets to the stones. The sound was almost musical.

"Does Alfheim always look like this?" I asked. Wonder had crept into my mind despite my best efforts.

Aidan strode beside me, glancing at the canopy above. "It forms to meet the expectations of those who enter. You expected a forest, so Alfheim provided. I blame those movies that people still watch, to be honest."

"Interesting." I took in the seamless way the world seemed to bend to my subconscious whims.

"Indeed. It also falls to us, the elves, to deal with the Formless ones. They are akin to us in essence," Aidan said, a note of solemnity creeping into his usually light tone.

"Formless Ones?" I said. I'd heard about the enemy, of course, the creatures who possessed Franklin with his consent after he was exiled from earth by my sister. Not from this source though, and the more I knew about them the better the whole of us could fight them.

"They are creatures of pure magic, without fixed shape or form. A sort of... cousin to our kind," he said, and I sensed there was much left unsaid.

We continued walking. My stomach rumbled, and my thoughts drifted to more mundane matters. "So, how do you farm here? Or is it a strictly carnivore diet? I know you like to hunt."

Aidan shook his head, the light stroking his blond hair. It was like this place loved him, which knowing Dream could manifest in a human form, I wasn't going to rule out. "No farms. Here, we conjure what we desire directly from the ether. Food, clothing, shelter, all is but a thought away. Which, since it requires no effort, makes it without any real value."

"Must be nice," I said. It sounded too good to be true, a life where your every want could materialize out of thin air. His comment about value made me wonder what drove the elves, since they had a paradise here.

"Indeed, it is one of the virtues of Alfheim," Aidan said. There was a trace of an emotion I couldn't identify in his tone that made me look over at him. He returned my attention with a half-smile, the kind that said he knew exactly what I was thinking.

We pressed on, the forest floor soft beneath my feet, the light from above filtered into a dance of shadows and sunbeams. Silence that had settled between us, strange but comfortable as we walked.

I put my finger on something nagging at me. There were no sounds of insects here.

The path curved, trending down, and Aiden paused as I hopped over an artistically fallen log. "Something that puzzled me about Earth is how so many people can't pursue the tasks they enjoy but have to work instead. Even though there is enough wealth and enough resources to do exactly that."

I snorted, the sound harsher than I intended. "Yeah, it sucks." My mind flitted to the countless hours I'd spent at less than fulfilling jobs, when

Repupair had first started and Franklin all but ran it into the ground. I'd supported us both.

He looked at me, his head tilted, curiosity lighting up his face. "What would you do if you were free? Truly free?"

I stopped walking and leaned against a tree, considering the question. I thought about the wedding plans sprawled across my living room table, the checklists, and first drafts of vendor contracts. "Honestly? Probably what I'm doing now, planning this insane wedding for Roma." I shrugged. "It's for my sister and that makes it worth it."

"Tell me, what tasks does this entail?" He seemed genuinely intrigued.

"Where do I start?" I ticked off on my fingers. "Catering, venue, music, invitations, floral arrangements, dress fittings, not to mention a dozen other things. Oh, and wrangling celebrity egos." I raised an eyebrow at him. "Then there's running after your people to make sure they don't create a disaster just for fun."

Aidan's expression flickered from interest to a look of bewilderment. "That sounds like... an impressive amount of responsibility. Though I don't really know what most of it entails."

"Story of my life." I laughed, then straightened and headed down the path. "But, if I could conjure up a five-tier wedding cake in five types of chocolate with a vegan counterpart with only a wave of my hand, I wouldn't be complaining it has no worth."

"Perhaps by the end of this, you might," he said, a considering expression on his face.

I let that comment lie. I didn't want to know, I had too much on my plate.

The forest became a grassy hill, the line separating them as sharp as if a ruler had drawn it.

On the rise of a hill stood a palace carved from white marble that gleamed like a signal against the backdrop of the verdant landscape. It was massive, its spires stretching skyward, each one tipped with what looked like gold, catching the sun in a dazzling display. Even with all Aiden had said about how easy it was to make things here, the beauty of it demanded my appreciation.

"Whoa," slipped from my lips before I could catch it.

Aiden, walking beside me, gave a small, proud smile. "I like this version too."

As we approached the grandeur of the elven architecture, a group of people on horses rode to meet us. The elves were imposing, decked in armor that seemed to ripple with an unseen force, their expressions stern and unreadable. Their big horses snorted, their hooves pawing at the ground before they too shimmered with that same uncanny energy.

I'd seen this before. Martellus called a gathering like this a warband and flatly said they were dangerous, to leave them be if I ever encountered elves like this.

"Lord Aiden." One of the warriors bowed from horseback.

"Commander," Aiden nodded back with a respectful tilt of his head. "Riding out? What threat?"

"Formless Ones pushing at the border." The commander's attention flicked to me briefly, a flash of curiosity there and gone. "Who is this?"

"Cassie." Aiden motioned toward me. "She's here to confirm her position as liaison with the King."

"Human?" The elf's eyebrow arched in surprise, but he offered a curt nod. "Welcome."

"Thanks." I was out of my depth but not willing to show it.

With a salute, the commander turned his mount, and the entire company of elves followed suit. In a matter of seconds, they spurred their horses into a gallop, and as if they were made of mist, they dissolved into nothingness, leaving only the clear sky above us.

"Did they just...?" I pointed upwards, incredulous.

"Vanish? Yes," Aiden said, his attention returning to the palace. "We have ways of traveling fast when we need to."

"Handy trick," I said under my breath, thinking of how convenient it would have been to fade away from problems back home over the years.

"Come." Aiden beckoned me forward. "Let's not keep my father waiting."

"Right, because that's not intimidating at all." I kept pace with him. Anxiety prickled through me. What was elven royalty like? I'd asked once and both Bran and Martellus had groaned as if dealing with them was a horrible burden, but never said why. Squaring my shoulders I projected confidence. Whatever came next, I could deal with it.

The grand arched entrance of the palace, a marvel of opulence, made me pause to marvel at it. The walls were lined with vivid tapestries, the scenes on them so realistic I felt I could touch the horses and feel the warmth under my fingertips. The floors gleamed as if they'd been polished just seconds ago. Yet, as I looked around, not a single person, servant or otherwise, could be seen maintaining the impeccable state of the place.

"Where is everyone?" Echoes mocked my words. "Who cleans all this?"

Aiden glanced back at me, his expression amused. "Magic takes care of the mundane tasks here. No servants are needed for such things."

"Magic for housekeeping. How convenient." I said more to myself than to him, imagining how different life would be if I could just wave away dirt and clutter.

"It is. Energy is saved for other pursuits." Innuendo wrapped the words as he gave me a long look, traveling from my boots to my face.

I blinked back at him and gave him a polite but puzzled expression. That had been spectacularly unsubtle.

Aiden laughed. I couldn't help my smile at the sound, and he offered me his arm. Taking it, I continued in silence until we reached massive double doors carved with intricate geometric designs that shifted and moved as I stared.

"Don't stare at them too long, they can have strange effects on humans," Aiden said as he pushed them open without effort, and we stepped into the throne room.

The ceiling was lost somewhere above us, hidden by the soft blue light filtering down. On a dais at the far end of the room, an elf lounged who bore a striking facial resemblance to Aiden. He slouched on the throne, one leg draped over the armrest, looking thoroughly bored. As we approached, his posture shifted, and he stood up so quickly it was as if he'd been jolted awake by an unseen current.

"Aiden," he exclaimed, his face brightening with a smile that transformed his entire demeanor.

"Father," Aiden said, and they embraced briefly, a gesture that seemed to carry genuine affection.

I stood awkwardly to the side, taking in the familial scene and wondering what sort of politics played out in these halls. Or if elves bothered with politics.

Chaotic as they seemed to be, why did they even have a king?

The two of them broke apart, turning toward me. My heart thumped, but I clamped down on my nerves. It was not the time to be nervous.

"May I present Cassandra Quinn." Aiden gestured toward me.

“Cassie, this is our King, Sloane Brighthand."

The king fixed his attention on me. Like Aiden, his eyes were a piercing blue, like looking into the heart of an eternal glacier. Cold and heavy and old, his gaze made my anxiety perk right up. A flicker of curiosity lightened his gaze before he offered a nod that seemed to convey both welcome and assessment in equal measure.

"An honor," I said, a bit steadier than I felt.

"Welcome to Alfheim, Cassandra," said the King. He examined me, without the flicker of innuendo Aiden had shown, like I was an interesting piece or art or a horse he was curious about. Neutral but attentive.

Aiden cleared his throat, drawing our attention to the matter at hand. "Sire, there is a situation with some of our kin on Earth. They're enjoying themselves, and not acknowledging Cassie's authority, given to her by me."

"Earth-drunk people can be... difficult." The king's lips twitched with amusement. Better you than me, his expression implied.

"Exactly," Aiden said, "so I've agreed to assist Cassie in managing them. We need them to understand she speaks with Your backing."

"Ah," Sloane nodded slowly. "So, you are the human who made that bargain with my son, Cassandra?"

"I am," I said, responsibility settling uncomfortably on my shoulders.

"Could you make it a royal decree, then, Sire?" Aiden asked. The casualness in his tone didn't match the request. He looked at me briefly, an unspoken promise that he was serious about this alliance.

The king smiled, the expression reaching his eyes. The color had shifted to an even more blazing blue. It really was like standing in a movie with a CGI team at the ready. "A royal decree, my son?" he said, as if savoring the words. "Of course."

He snapped his fingers, and instantly I felt a shift in the air around me. It was like the softest shawl had settled on my shoulders, warm and light. Looking down at myself, I noticed a faint shimmer, like sunlight glinting off morning dew. It reminded me of the magic just before Aiden and I passed through the gate.

"From now on, you'll be seen in a different light, Cassie," Sloane said with a note of finality. "Quite literally."

After the decree was made, a deepening hush fell upon the throne room. I watched, barely daring to breathe as the king rose from his throne and turned toward Aiden. His movements were deliberate, each step carrying ceremony.

"Son. Aiden," he said with a gravity that seemed to pull at the very air, "you have shown the wisdom and strength required of a ruler. You are ready."

Before I could process what was happening, Sloane removed the crown from his head, a simple circlet that held the light of countless stars and placed it atop Aiden's brow. He then bowed deeply, a gesture of profound respect and surrender.

"Your Majesty." He straightened up to look Aiden in the face. A light of unholy laughter had entered his own,

"Father?" Aiden's voice, normally rich, musical and confident, was almost a squawk. It held a note of disbelief, his usual confidence momentarily replaced by vulnerability.

Laughter bubbled up from Sloane, ex-king, rich and warm, chasing away the hush. "You'll do a great job. Now, I'm retired. It's time for me to find some fun."

The twinkle in his eyes made me very nervous. What was 'fun' for an elf king? Even one that had stepped down?

With a joyful bounce in his step, Sloane Brighthand turned on his heel and strode away from us.

The hall rang with his command. "Bring me my armor."

Beside me, Aiden let out a long sigh. He took the crown off and twirled it on a finger. Catching my eyes, he offered a wry, lopsided grin. "See what I have to deal with?"

I watched Sloane's retreating figure, then turned back to Aiden, whose expression was resignation and amusement. The absurdity of it all hit me, a coronation and abdication within the span of heartbeats, and here I was, a human wrapped in elf magic, standing witness in the most casual outfit ever.

They were all insane. At the moment it was an endearing madness, a freedom I found myself inexplicably drawn to.

“Let’s head back to earth, then,” said Aiden. I took his offered hand.

4
AIDEN

The ground beneath our feet solidified, and as we stood on Earth the veil closed behind us. Cassie's hazel eyes, wide and confused and amused just moments ago, now took in the familiar surroundings with a touch of relief. She turned to me, her raven-black hair cascading over her shoulders in waves that any ocean would envy.

"Shouldn't you go back and start running your kingdom or something?" Cassie asked, her tone laced with responsibility, a trait sorely lacking among my kind. Her serious tone prodded two urges, pausing to enjoy the refreshing draft of concern, and a nigh irresistible urge to act in the opposite direction.

"Let them come find me if they need their king." I shrugged. The magic that marked my ascension was not subtle; it had echoed across all the realms with an elf in them. "For now, I find the company of a human planning the wedding of another king far too intriguing to abandon."

Her lips quirked up at the corners, even as her brows furrowed, the perfect blend of accepted flattery and skepticism.

"Eventually, though," I said, "duty will call me back." Not yet. Not while Cassie's fiery spirit and unexplored depths remained new and fresh.

"Where are we?" she asked, looking from brick buildings to trees to street.

"Close to the source of your recent change in fortune." I nodded toward a nondescript building nearby. I'd followed the magical signature of Luck, now called Ms. Fortuna. I wanted to see what might happen if they met, gain more information on if the turn of her luck was fair or foul.

Cassie sighed. "Words Aiden, explain further, I have no idea what you're talking about, and I need to get back to work again."

Despite that, her gaze traveled on the street, her curiosity piqued.

“A...person I know contacted me and told me your luck was about to change. Her residence is near. I hope to find out more of what she meant. She’s often cryptic."

Cassie said, “Takes one to know one." Interest filled her triangular face.

The game was afoot, and whether she admitted it or not, she was every bit curious as I was. Then she shook her head briskly.

"No. I need to get back to work. Thanks for the lift," Cassie said, briskly brushing off the remnants of trans-dimensional travel from her clothes, a curious mixture of stardust and earthly grit. "But I've got a wedding to plan, and a list longer than ... I don’t know what. Something long. Are you now going to keep your elvish entourage from interrupting?"

"Me? Run herd on the elves?" I raised an eyebrow. "Isn't that part of your other job as the liaison? Besides, shouldn't you be with me to guide them? You know better than I what is acceptable and what is not in this world at this time."

"Guide them?" Cassie chuckled, the sound rich and warm despite the edge of incredulity. "I can barely keep up with the weird stuff they do. If you want to know what's acceptable, you should ask Rey. He's practically written the book on human behavior, or so he claims."

"Rey?" I scoffed lightly, though a part of me considered the suggestion for an instant before dismissing it. The trickster king was as likely to lead me into a prank as he was to give genuine advice. "You're full of jokes today."

"Hey, I'm just trying to help," she said, still laughing. The sound danced around us, light and happy. She dialed a number on her phone, her focus shifting to it, leaving me a moment to ponder the notion of seeking counsel from Rey.

If he pranked me, I could do it right back. A war with Rey would certainly not be dull. There didn't seem a downside to it once I started considering it.

Maybe it wouldn't be the worst idea. After all, understanding humans seemed crucial, especially if I intended to stick around Cassie without causing a magical incident. Rey, with his compulsion for mischief, might provide some insight. Or at least, we'd both be entertained.

Cassie shot me a sharp look when she ended her call. "You're smiling. What are you planning, Aiden?"

"Only more ways to see that spark in your eyes," I said with a grin. "Anger becomes you."

"Flattery will get you nowhere," she said, but her lips twitched into a reluctant smile. "Why aren't you planning to go home and run your kingdom?"

Her question, stated in a serious tone, hung between us. I shrugged. "My kingdom runs itself for the most part. If my people need me, they'll find me."

She shook her head, frowning. "That's a pretty cavalier attitude for a king."

"Carefree, perhaps," I said. "It gives me time for more... pleasant pursuits." Her cheeks flushed, the annoyance dancing in her hazel eyes battling with amusement.

"Charming," she deadpanned. "If I were a damsel, I'd be sure to swoon at your feet."

"Don't want one." I stepped closer. "I'm far more interested in the woman who stands before me, all layers and complications."

"Keep dreaming, Your Majesty," Cassie said, but conflict flickered her stern facade. It was clear she was enjoying our banter as much as I was, and equally clear she was conflicted about it.

"Speaking of dreams," I said, "I was hoping to accompany you—"

"Accompany me?" Cassie looked around. "To where? The dentist office we're standing in front of? Do elves get cavities?"

"We don't," I said with a dismissive wave. "To answer your worry before you deflect more, elves are resourceful. If there's trouble, they'll figure out how to reach me. It's not my job to make myself readily available to them."

"Convenient, this style of rulership," Cassie said dryly. "What's the real reason you want to tag along with me?"

I leaned in, close enough to see the flecks of gold in her eyes. "Curiosity," I said. "Perhaps, the chance for entertainment. You're never boring."

Her laughter rang out again, genuine and unguarded. "I suppose I could use the company. Remember, nothing disruptive. We're doing this the efficient way."

"Agreed." I offered her my arm. "Shall we?"

She took my arm with a shake of her head. "This should be interesting. However, the wedding planning isn't going to pause for elvish whims."

Cassie paused, her free hands on her hip, exuding that fascinating fire.

Wedding planning seemed dreadfully mundane compared to the adventures we could be having. I was willing to accept the restrictions to enjoy her company.

"Understood. I'll abide by your priorities." I nodded, keeping my tone light, despite the pang of disappointment.

The air beside us shimmered, and my sister Matilda appeared as if stepping out from behind an invisible curtain. She patted the flowing draperies she wore and grinned, bright enough to distract the driver on the street near us and nearly cause an accident.

Cassie jumped, surprise in every line of her body.

"Can elves—" she said, then trailed off, seemingly lost in thought about the implications of invisibility.

"Matilda." I flourished a bow to my sister, though being king I shouldn't. "A fine dramatic entrance."

"Found you," Matilda said with a smirk. "Thought you might be up to something fun."

"Matilda, you and Cassie have met," I reintroduced them, eager to see how Cassie would react to another of my kind now that she knew us better.

"Good to see you again," Cassie said cautiously.

"Likewise. So, would you care to join us, Aiden? We've found a volcano in one of the big oceans that's just begging for a little encouragement," Matilda asked.

"Absolutely not." Cassie stiffened, sending me a glare that could melt steel. "We're not encouraging volcanoes or causing any other natural disasters today, thank you very much."

"Matilda, that would be better another day," I said quickly, hoping to soothe the situation.

"As you wish, my king," Matilda said with a playful pout, turning her attention back to Cassie. "But you must admit, it does sound like fun."

"Not the word I'd use," Cassie said, her tone suggesting that the conversation was over.

"Indeed." I gave my sister a pointed look. "I will be with Cassie for the rest of the day. I am aiding in the wedding preparations for the Goblin King's nuptials."

Cassie closed her eyes.

"The Location is Fellmere Island. We will leave for that destination tomorrow," Cassie said, with a new firmness in her voice that commanded attention. I nodded, appreciating her attitude.

"Sounds like a plan," I said casually. Behind Cassie, clearly visible to me, Luck slipped into a low brick building across the street. In the shadows of the alley next to the building, a familiar presence revealed itself. Halo, with her stealth and predatory grace, lurked. Her attention was divided between me and Cassie.

The cat goddess's memory and tendency to revenge wasn't one to take lightly but given circumstances I gave her the benefit of the doubt. Perhaps she intended to let bygones be bygones.

With a nonchalant wave in her direction, I called out, "Hey, Halo." I flashed a grin at her expression before focusing back on Cassie and Matilda.

"Are we just going to stand here then?" Matilda asked, obviously itching for something more exciting than wedding plans, even though they were for a fellow king.

"If you want interim entertainment." I reached into the ether and pulling out my fiddle. "I've got a better idea."

Cassie watched, wary and curious as the instrument materialized in my hands. "What are you doing?"

"Improving the ambiance." I placed the fiddle under my chin. A few experimental strokes of the bow and the rich, sweet notes filled the air. People on the street began to turn heads, drawn by the sudden music.

"Here?" Cassie looked around, clearly surprised by my impromptu performance.

"Why not?" I asked. "These people need a touch of beauty in their lives, a spark of magic to lift them from the mundane."

"Only you would think busking is magic." Cassie shook her head, but there was no anger in her voice, just a blend of amusement and wistfulness.

The lady wanted a kind of magic lacking in her life, though she did have love. Which was its own magic, one that elves weren't very good at.

As my melody rippled through the air, the world transformed. Faces softened, steps slowed, and the ordinary became extraordinary.

The fiddle sang, a wild tune that echoed between the dust, engine fumes and blocky buildings and danced along the lives on the bustling sidewalks. My fingers moved with practiced ease, drawing out a melody that spoke of ancient forests and starlit nights.

Matilda didn't resist the call of my music. With a swirl of her skirts, she moved into an open spot on the pavement. Her feet flowed on the concrete, perfectly in sync with the music. She swayed and spun, her movements as fluid as the notes themselves, attracting a circle of onlookers.

Cassie's eyes flicked from me to Matilda to the crowd, and her lips curved gently upward. Moments past as she swayed as well, caught in the simple spell of music.

Then her gaze jerked back to me, wide with alarm.

"Stop," Cassie said. "Aiden, stop playing."

Confusion furrowed my brow as I drew my bow across the strings softening the music so I could speak. The melody hung in the air, quivering like a leaf about to fall.

"What's wrong?" I asked, looking around.

The crowd pressed in, hands reaching forward holding crumpled bills, tossing them into my fiddle's case on the ground.

"Enough." Cassie's command was sharp, her petite frame pushing against the tide of bodies. "Stop, Aiden."

I lowered the fiddle, the wood warm under my fingers. "Why are they brandishing money?"

"Because that's what you do when someone busks!" Cassie exclaimed, her tone blending frustration and laughter.

Matilda bowed to the people pressing forward, then retreated to my side.

"Busks?" I said. The word was unfamiliar.

"Street performing." She stepped back by me, stopping her attempts to stem the flow of coins and notes into my case. "It draws a crowd... and this is too much attention. Roma won't be happy, especially if it causes a traffic problem."

"Ah," I said, finally grasping the situation.

"No more," I said. "We play and dance no more today. Please move on with your lives." I wove a subtle command into the words, and people began to move away rather than pressing forward.

When they'd cleared, I reached down to help Cassie gather the scattered bills. "We need a larger area, then?"

"Maybe," she said. Her dark hair swung as she scooped up a handful of bills, waving them at me like some sort of bizarre fan. "Seriously, Aiden, what on earth are we going to do with this?"

"Isn't it customary to keep such tokens of appreciation?" I asked, genuinely puzzled by the human custom. Money served in many ways, apparently.

"Tokens of appreciation?" She let out a laugh that was half irritation, half genuine mirth. "No, we don't need money. We're not street performers."

"Why now perform on the streets?" asked Matilda, tilting her head in puzzlement.

"Because you don't need the money." Cassie's hands went to her hips, and she shook her head. "Look, just donate it. There's a charity box at the coffee shop around the corner. Give it to them."

Matilda brows rose and an interested look crossed her face.

"Very well," I said, though the idea seemed odd. Why keep charity in a box? If we put money in, would garments fall out for another person? Was the box full of the essence of charity or the act of charity?

"Next time you feel the urge to play," Cassie said, a quiet wistful tone in her voice, "maybe just play for me? Not out here."

"Ah, for your ears alone," I said, already the notes and chords of a new melody twining through my thoughts, a song inspired only by Cassie. I nodded, tucking the fiddle under my arm, ready to follow her lead. The spark in her eyes promised more adventures to come, and I found myself looking forward to each and every one.

I pocketed the fiddle just as a human male extended a slip of paper toward my sister, digits scrawled on it in hasty ink. Matilda, curious but trying to be polite to keep Cassie happy, and by extension me, glanced at me with a shrug that seemed to say, "What now?"

She accepted the coded note, and he appeared triumphant as he melted back into the thinning crowd.

A flash of red caught my notice. A car pulling up to the curb with a familiar fiery-haired driver.

"Rey's Cathy," Matilda said, recognition lighting

her features. "The trickster's mate. Is she fair game to play?"

"Not until we know her strength," I said.

Cathy jumped out, a whirlwind of energy and purpose and darted into the alley. She latched onto the arm of a grumpy-looking Halo, and with a determined tug, Cathy began to march them both toward a nearby low brick building, its discreet sign above reading 'MDS'.

"Hey, Cassie!" Cathy called over her shoulder, her voice ringing with that trademark sarcasm. "Good you're here. You didn't answer my text, so elf coincidence is a great thing. Come on. Shay thinks a visit will be good for you."

Cassie puffed a sigh between pursed lips but couldn't hide the twitch of amusement at their corners. "Fine, but this is strictly observational."

"Of course," Cathy said, though her tone suggested otherwise.

"Looks like we're taking a detour," I said to Matilda, motioning toward the procession.

"Observational," Matilda said, her tone interested, her attention piqued. "Let us observe as well."

We fell into step behind Cassie, our little group an odd mix of reluctance and curiosity, heading into whatever havoc Cathy had in store for us next.

Stepping into the 'MDS' building was disappointing. It appeared to me a very average office, not some place the Trickster King's mate would drag his unwilling second. I'd expected an arena or a contest, perhaps a giant or two.

Not even a person at the desk marked 'receptionist'.

Halo's glare could sour milk. So, there must be something interesting here.

"Really? This is what we're doing now?" she said, sarcasm an almost palpable presence around her. "I have so many gaps in my endlessly exciting schedule for dates you feel a need to fill them?"

Cassie folded her arms across her chest, her stance unhappy. "This is the place Roma used?" she asked. "I'm not looking for another relationship."

"Shay suggested you come here," Cathy said with a shrug. "You know Shay when she makes a statement. So, suck it up, buttercup."

I tilted my head slightly, catching Cassie's attention. "What's wrong?" I asked. "What is this place?"

"A dating service for magical beings. It brings you love," she snorted, the word escaping like a curse, but with the hint of tears behind it. “Not something I want."

“Why?" asked Matilda, her voice soft and gentle. We could both tell Cassie wanted to speak of what troubled her, but pain blocked the words. A glance at Cathy discovered an expression of sadness, while Halo had reverted to an indifferent expression.

In this context, the cat-goddess was wroth and looking for a reason to claw a target to shreds, either with her hands or her tongue.

She said nothing, the air loaded with Matilda's gentle suggestion to Cassie to speak.

"My ex-husband, Franklin, he..." Cassie hesitated, chewing on her full lower lip before continuing.

"He used love elixirs to keep me from divorcing him when I found out he'd been unfaithful with lots of different women. Made me forgive him and want him to stay. Then, when he had an opportunity, he tried to arrange a threesome with me and my sister, Roma. I don't want a man in my life if that's what I attract."

"Roma? The Goblin king's mate? Does this man still live?" I asked.

Difficult to redress her hurt if the man were dead.

"Yes. That worm used her, too." She spat out 'worm' like it was venom. "He stole her magic. Took it to make his own better. He hurt her."

I regarded her. The man still lived, which gave me an opportunity to deal with this...vermin. "Your anger is most justified," I said quietly.

Humans rarely surprised me with their capacity for cruelty, but this...this was a new depth.

"Did Franklin force you to sleep with him?" I asked, keeping my tone gentle and reassuring. My hands had curled into fists, the knuckles bone white.

Matilda was frowning as well.

Cathy's eyes were sad. Halo, her gaze on my hands, smiled, white teeth gleaming.

Cassie paused, averting her eyes and shaking her head. "No, after the first potion, we didn't... He had lots of girlfriends to keep him occupied, which is partially why I wanted the divorce."

The old pain in her voice made me wish to harm this Franklin the worm to collect her pain back threefold.

"He pressed your sister to be his mistress as well?" The act of a fool, true.

"Yes." She shuddered visibly at the thought. "Sometimes I wonder... If there hadn't been other women available, would he have used me as a convenience?" The question hung heavily in the air between us.

Cathy's expression had darkened. Halo remained expressionless.

Anger boiled in me, hot and potent. The idea of someone hurting Cassie, damaging her in such a way ignited pure rage. How dare this man harm the woman I wanted?

"I'd be more than happy to deal with this worm for you." The words came out before I considered if they'd frighten her. "Really, no trouble at all. Would you like his head fresh or dried?"

I clamped down on further words, expecting horror or perhaps fear at my offer. Instead, Cassie's laughter caught me off-guard, bright and unexpectedly buoyant.

"No," she chuckled, shaking her head as if casting away darkness. "Diamonds are better."

The bright grin she gave is all outshone any precious stone I could imagine as she firmly changed the course of the conversation. "And Franklin is in the past, too, so I'd like to move on."

Her words struck a chord within me. Here was a woman who had faced betrayal and manipulation yet chose to laugh and enjoy the now. It was a moment of clarity, seeing how close she could be in thought to an elf.

"As you will," I said. "Let's focus on the future, shall we?"

"An excellent idea," said Luck, also known as Ms. Fortuna, from the hallway leading further into the building.

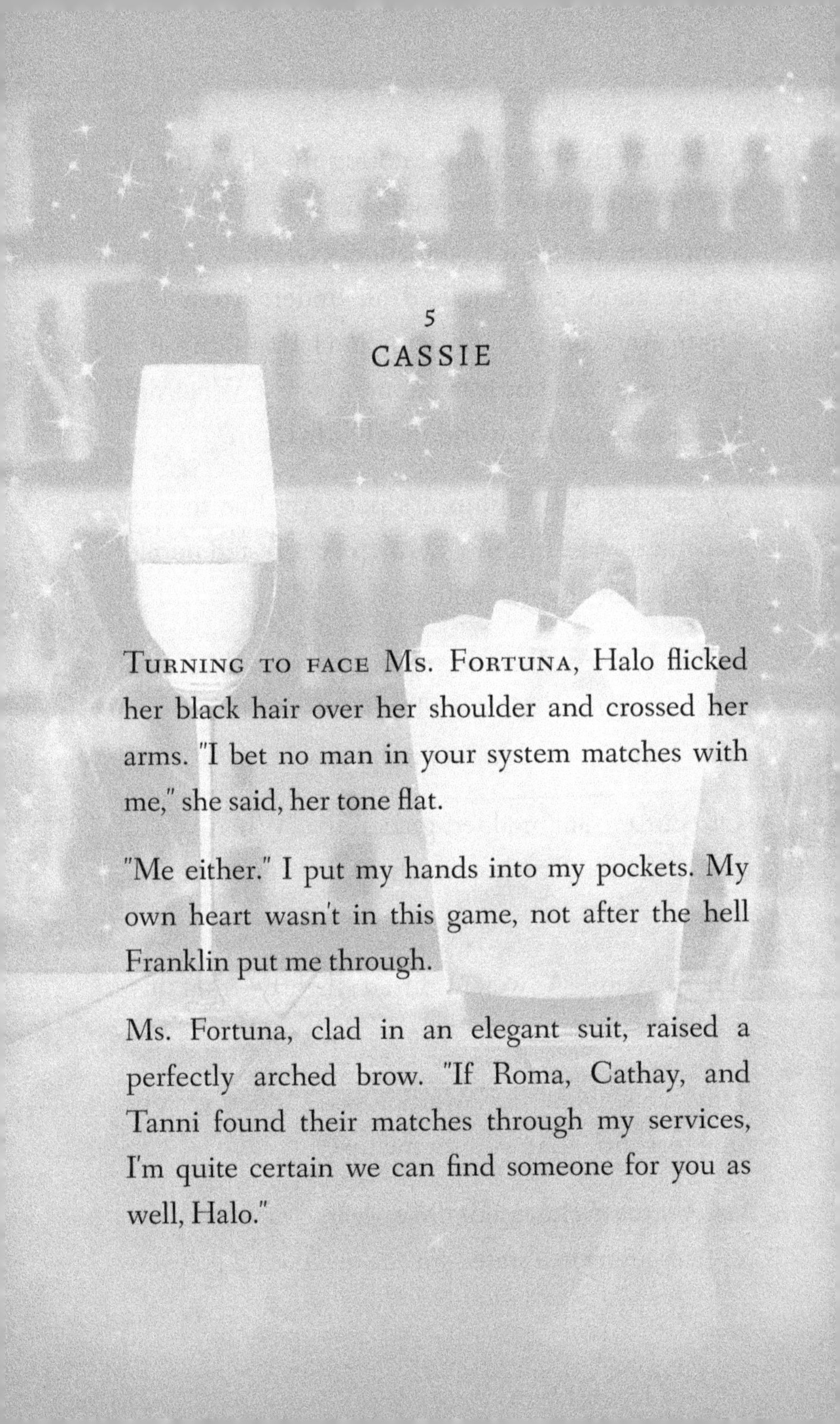

5

CASSIE

Turning to face Ms. Fortuna, Halo flicked her black hair over her shoulder and crossed her arms. "I bet no man in your system matches with me," she said, her tone flat.

"Me either." I put my hands into my pockets. My own heart wasn't in this game, not after the hell Franklin put me through.

Ms. Fortuna, clad in an elegant suit, raised a perfectly arched brow. "If Roma, Cathay, and Tanni found their matches through my services, I'm quite certain we can find someone for you as well, Halo."

I watched their exchange, noting the slight tilt of Ms. Fortuna's head, the enigmatic glint in her eyes. Something in the way she addressed Halo caught my attention, and I sensed an undercurrent of... what? Amusement? Anticipation? I couldn't put my finger on it, but it made me uneasy. What did she know about the world that I didn't?

"As for you, Ms. Quinn, it's perfectly fine to take your time." Ms. Fortuna's brown eyes rested on me with a gentler expression.

I managed a half-smile, tucking a strand of hair behind my ear. "Maybe I'll take the tests later," I said. "Just... not today. Not right now."

"Of course." She nodded gracefully. "When you're ready, if ever, I'm here to help. No pressure, no rush."

"Thank you." A weight lifted slightly from my shoulders.

"Hey, what about me?" Matilda said suddenly, stepping forward. "Can you set me up?"

Ms. Fortuna chuckled. "My dear, I'm afraid my services aren't calibrated for the elven kind just yet.

Come back in a year and a day, when I have time to change the parameters needed."

Matilda shrugged, seemingly unfazed, and wandered toward the door. "No worries, I'll find my own fun," she called over her shoulder.

I watched her go, a knot forming in my stomach. Where was she off to? Something about Matilda's casual departure stirred a sense of paranoia within me. Based on my recent experiences with elves it was entirely justified.

Halo flashed a grin with a dark sardonic undernote. "Wish me luck," she said, though it was clear she felt she didn't need it.

As the door closed behind her, I turned to find Aiden examining the various trinkets and framed certificates on the walls with a detached curiosity. I remained standing, shifting from one foot to the other.

"So how are the wedding ideas coming?" Cathy asked. She was leaning against the desk, flipping through a bridal magazine with a critical expression.

"Not too bad." I clasped my hands behind my back. "It's a lot of planning for something this large."

"True. Going to be one heck of a party. " Cathy's sudden grin sparkled with mischief, and I cracked a smile in answer.

"Speaking of which, what is customary attire for these events?" Aiden asked, pivoting toward us from the wall.

"Usually, it's whatever makes the bride look like a goddess and the groom slightly uncomfortable in a tux," Cathy said, and I snorted at the accuracy.

"A bit lacking in detail," Aiden said dryly, but with amusement in his eyes. "Any interesting practices? Anything I should prepare for?"

"Depends on the couple, really," I said. "In this case, you can't go wrong so long as everyone knows you're wearing your best."

"My best?" he said.

"Your best," Cathy said with a nod, closing the magazine and tossing it back onto the pile. "Though be ready for it to be rowdy, especially if there's an open bar."

“What do these affairs look like?" he asked.

"Imagine a sea of flowers," Cathy said, her hands weaving through the air as if she could pluck the petals from an invisible bouquet. "White roses, lilies, some peonies for good measure."

"Peonies are nice." I pictured the lush blooms.

"Tables draped in silk, candles flickering everywhere," she said. "In the middle of it all, the couple, dancing their first dance on a floor that looks like it's made of stars."

Aiden nodded, eyes intent, and I felt a little uneasy.

"Not real stars," I hastened to add. “There’s a lot of details to organize, as I told you before. All these details add up to expense."

"Expensive, but worth it for some," Cathy said with a sigh. "It's all about that moment, you know? When everything else falls away and it's just the two of them."

Since I knew for a fact Rey would marry Cathy in a heartbeat if she expressed the desire, I didn’t comment.

“When are you checking out the venue? Shay’s island?" Cathy asked.

"I’ll be flying out of Logan tomorrow. Aiden, since you wanted to go, if there's room, I can try to get you on the same flight."

"Logan? Logan what?" Aiden asked.

"It’s an airport," I said with a twinge of something warm at the idea of traveling with him. "I'll check on availability when I get home."

"My thanks," he said with a nod. "Traveling together would be pleasant."

The door opened, and Halo stepped out, an irritated expression on her face. "Well, that was as fun as watching paint dry."

"Fun?" I said.

"Do you want to take your turn, Cassie?" she asked. The sarcasm in her voice intensified. "You can't dodge Cupid's arrow forever."

"Who says I'm dodging? Perhaps I'm just... strategically retreating." I tried to match her tone despite the heaviness settling in my chest.

We headed out the door, Aiden shutting it behind us. He waved as he strode toward the small park at the end of the street.

I continued to the car with Cathy and Halo.

"But you can't run from love forever, Cass." Cathy said mildly, unlocking the car with a beep.

"Watch me," I said under my breath as we opened the doors.

Cathy shot me a knowing look but didn't press further.

"Let's get you both home." She started the engine.

"Thank you, O my queen." Halo said, leaned back in her seat.

"Thanks Cathy," I said with a strange mix of relief and disappointment as we pulled away from MDS.

Aiden gave a small wave from the sidewalk as we passed him, his figure growing smaller until he was just another face in the crowd headed for the park.

I hoped I wouldn't get a call about an emergency any time soon.

"See you later, Aiden," I said quietly, even though he was far beyond earshot now.

"Thinking about that airport rendezvous already?" Cathy asked, catching my gaze in the rearview mirror.

"Possibly," I said.

"Good." She smiled back. "I can hope. But I'm not sure an elf is the best choice for starting out again."

As the city passed by outside the window, I let my mind wander to the possibilities ahead, wondering whether Cathy was right.

6
CASSIE

SUNLIGHT CREPT THROUGH THE BLINDS, casting stripes across my living room floor. Getting tickets to fly last night for Aiden had been a complete bust due to lack of ID, since Rey wasn't able to provide it quite that fast. I simply hadn't thought of it before I offered.

I needed to explain it to him.

A knock at the door jolted me upright while tying my sneakers. I peered through the peephole to see Aiden on the other side, waving in the direction of the glass.

I swung the door open. He looked past me, scanning the interior of my apartment as if searching for hidden answers.

"Cassie." He shifted his weight, a touch of uncertainty in his stance.

"Morning, Aiden. What's wrong?" I asked, leaning against the doorframe with arms folded.

"Your... what did you call it? Airplane? I spoke with the trickster king. You confine yourself in a metal tube and breathe stale air for hours on end to travel?" He rubbed the back of his neck, looking horrified. "It sounds terrible."

I couldn't suppress a chuckle. He was trying and failing to be tactful. "Welcome to human travel. Luckily, you don't have to worry about it this time."

"Go on," he beckoned me to continue.

"Items that we don't have for you are required. You'll need to get there on your own. What do you need to navigate?" I asked.

"A picture will do."

I sighed in internal relief. That I had. I walked to my laptop and pulled up a picture of the island, then a global map as well.

He stared at it and then nodded. “Yes, I can ride there."

Apparently, elf horses could fly long distances. I’d find out how fast soon.

"Where's your sister?" I changed the subject. The mention of her seemed to shift something in his demeanor; a wry expression crossed his face.

"Ah, she's... running an errand for me." Aiden avoided eye contact, focusing instead on a nearby potted plant.

"Really, now?" I pursed my lips. "Why do I get the feeling you're not telling me everything?"

He met my gaze then, a half-smile playing on his lips. "Because you're perceptive. I may have sent her off deliberately to enjoy the company of a band in the western ocean. I wanted some time alone with you, without the biggest gossip in three realms listening in."

"Is that right?" I leaned closer, intrigued by his candid admission. Alarms rang in my head, suggesting strongly I lean back

"Indeed," he said, his gaze holding mine with an intensity that suggested more than just a desire for privacy.

"Okay." I got up from the couch. "I have to go and board the human way of flying."

"You could ride with me," he said tentatively.

I LAUGHED, but it didn't quite mask the flutter in my chest. " Aiden, you do realize humans can't just zip through the air flying, right? We need planes... and oxygen."

"Ah," he said, the word drawn out as if he were considering an irritating obstacle. "Yes, that would pose a challenge. I believe I can find a way around it, given thought. May I attend you as you proceed to the airport?"

"Sure. Just don't do any flying anywhere near the planes." The weight of reality settled back on me. Elves and their powerful magic, there was no future in getting caught up in that.

At the airport, Aiden's intent eyes swept over the bustling terminal.

"You can't go further than here," I said at the first checkpoint. He nodded and strode away, back toward the entrance.

I frowned, watching his retreating back. Shaking my head, I joined the security line, digging for my ID while my thoughts wandered to all the potential trouble he could get into. It was a horrifying list.

The airplane seat felt stiff against my back as I settled in, but my attention was outside the window. The plane taxied and lifted off. When it leveled out, there he was, Aiden pacing alongside near my window, his ethereal horse matching our speed effortlessly. It was surreal, seeing them unaffected by the whipping wind, almost like a scene pulled from a dream.

People gasped and stared.

I couldn't help but smile. He seemed so focused, so intent on staying nearby. His features, sharp and elegant, held a kind of wild beauty that called to the heart. Despite myself, I imagined what it might be like to explore something more with him, something deeper.

My sister had found happiness; could I dare try again and hope for the same?

"Down, Cassie," I said. "One step at a time."

A movie, a nap and a few extra hours later, Aiden swerved away as the pilot announced we were descending.

The wheels of the plane stopped. Unbuckling my seatbelt, I grabbed my carry-on bag from the overhead compartment, feeling the latent energy of the flight humming in my bones. As I shuffled down the aisle alongside weary travelers, I looked for Aiden.

Had he circumvented security, or would he be in the waiting area? Where would he hide his horse?

"Intent" was the word that came to mind when I thought about Aiden. He hadn't pushed or prodded since I'd opened up about my past with Franklin. Instead, he had hovered, quite literally at times, in ways that made me feel like he was there because he wanted to be, not because he expected anything in return. The realization brought a warmth that contrasted sharply with my feelings of misery about relationships.

I stepped through the aircraft doorway and into the chilly embrace of English weather. Scanning the tarmac as I descended the stairs, I spotted Aiden, his horse, and security personnel rushing over.

I rushed to Aiden's side to avert disaster. Shay had foreseen something happening, and she'd had calls made. I just needed to invoke the right names to get the security to back away. Even still, it was a tense half hour before I could turn my attention back to him.

A storm was blowing in, the wind getting worse as I negotiated.

"You ready?" I asked, the question whipped away from my lips by the wind.

The helicopter, a spindly thing with blades that looked too flimsy against the storm's fury, swayed at its mooring. I took one look at it and felt my stomach churn. Aiden took my hand, his expression calm despite the tempest.

"Want to ride the wind on a different mount?" he asked, a playful edge to his voice.

"Have you come up with a way I'm not gasping for air or freezing the whole way?" I said, half-joking but entirely serious about not wanting to fly in this weather.

"Trust me," he said, a smile lifting the corners of his mouth. "I've put thought into it."

"Okay." I nodded, feeling a bit of trepidation but also trust. "Let's do it."

One risk. I'd take it.

I texted the transportation coordinator to let him know I'd found an alternative as the text arrived letting me know the flight was postponed due to weather.

Aiden whistled, a clear, sharp sound that interrupted the howling wind. For a moment, nothing happened, and I wondered if the horse would even hear us over the storm. Then, in a shimmer of light that seemed impossible given the darkening skies, his horse appeared, its form solidifying out of thin air.

"Meet Cu," Aiden said as he approached the spectral creature. Up close, it was majestic, more lovely than any horse I'd ever seen, with a coat and mane that seemed woven from moonlight.

"Hi, Cu." I reached out a tentative hand. The horse nuzzled into my palm, and something akin to laughter echoed in my mind.

"Ready?" Aiden asked, turning to offer me his hand.

"Let's hope so." I took a deep breath before placing my hand in his.

I was going to assume that his magic horse was not subject to all the reasons riding double without safety gear was a terrible idea. Since I'd seen it flying.

With Aiden's assistance, I swung my leg over Cu's back, settling behind Aiden. The horse's body was fever warm under me, an anchor amidst the gusts that whipped around us. As Aiden adjusted to make sure I was secure, I wrapped my arms around his waist and grabbed his belt, the reality of what we were about to do sinking in.

I had gone insane. Normal Cassie had left the building, risky Cassie was riding an elf horse.

"Keep your grip tight," Aiden said, and without another word, Calen leapt into the storm with us on his back.

The wind rushed past us, but it didn't lash at me as I feared. It was a caress, a gentle push against my face that brought with it the scent of rain and adventure. Below, London sprawled like a toy city, its iconic landmarks miniature beneath us. The Thames wound through it all like a silver ribbon.

"Is this real?" I asked, my words barely audible above the rushing air.

"As real as anything," Aiden said. His back was a solid wall against my chest, his muscles firm and reassuring.

I tightened my grip around him, noting the surprising warmth radiating from his body. It matched Cu's, both were like miniature furnaces. Probably helped with being unfazed by the altitude or the chill.

"Where does Cu come from?" I said, curiosity getting the better of me as we soared over the patchwork fields beyond the city.

"Elven horses are our friends and cousins. They choose their forms based on the bond they share with us," he said. "Their life is different from creatures of flesh and blood."

"How?" Cu's shimmering form moved with such grace and power. Also, he flew. A good hint he wasn't a non-magical creature.

"Magic and spirit give them power. Cu can be faster than any plane if he wishes." There was pride in his voice, a deep affection that told me of his connection to the creature carrying us.

"Elves are powerful. But you don't look... intimidating. Not like some of Bran's or Martellus' people." I kept my grip on his belt as his stomach muscles contracted on laughter.

"Ah, our current appearance. Once, we struck terror into the hearts of men, but expectations shape reality. The modern world sees elves as beautiful, so here we are." He chuckled again. "It has its moments now, though."

"Beautiful doesn't mean harmless, though," I said, thinking of the strength I could feel under my hands.

"Indeed," he said, a hint of something darker in his tone. "Beauty can be deceiving."

Cu banked sharply, the motion effortless, and we were suspended over an endless sea of green, the world holding its breath with us. For that infinite second, I forgot everything but the wonder of flight.

Aiden shifted slightly, and the motion drew my attention away from the sprawling landscape below us. "Cassie, why have you never trained in your powers?" he asked over the rush of air.

"Because I don't really know what they are and haven't had much of a chance to practice since I found out I have them," I said, a little defensively.

"Would you want me to inquire about potential teachers? Perhaps there's an elf who remembers a human with similar abilities and how they used them." His hand rested on my arm, the touch soothing.

I was taken aback by his offer, but something about it felt right, like pieces of a puzzle clicking together. "Yes, I believe I would like that."

"Good," he nodded with satisfaction. Then he glanced back at me with a curious tilt of his head. "Do you prefer cats or dogs?"

"Both." I smiled despite the strangeness of the question. "I like both."

"Ah," he said, and Cu's ears twitched backward, as though he was listening in on our conversation.

The flight continued in comfortable silence, crossing a choppy sea, the rain somehow not getting us wet, until we descended toward a windswept island, where a small group awaited us under a small shelter near a landing pad for helicopters.

As we landed, a tall thin older man with a dignified posture stepped forward, his face breaking into a warm smile.

"Welcome, Miss Cassie. I'm Butler," he introduced himself.

I shook my head, amused. "Your name is Butler?"

He laughed, a rich sound that echoed against the stone of the nearby buildings. "Indeed, Miss. It's a common reaction, but I assure you, it's a name I bear with honor."

"Thank you, Butler," I said, relieved to be on solid ground and even more relieved to see that the presence of elves didn't faze the staff here.

"Cassie." Aiden dropped the saddlebags containing my luggage on the tarmac.

His expression changed as a faint, melodic ringtone sounded from his pocket. He pulled out a small mirror. "Excuse me one moment." He stepped aside and snapping a taut, "Yes?"

I watched him move away, his conversation muffled by the wind as I turned to Butler, feeling oddly grounded amidst this new world of magic.

Who knew elves had a phone equivalent?

“I’m going to stretch my legs then head for the castle in a couple minutes. Take the saddlebags, my luggage is inside them, and meet me there, please."

"Take care near the cliffs," Butler cautioned pointedly.

"Will do," I promised. My butt and stomach and thighs ached, and I wanted to stretch them a little. Fellmere Island unfolded before me like a scene from a movie. Quaint but quietly majestic. A heliport sat starkly to one side, its metallic sheen at odds with the land around it.

A small village huddled in the distance, a smattering of roofs peeking through greenery, while the castle loomed behind me, a silhouette cut from stone against the backdrop of roiling clouds.

A spit of rain hit me. My footsteps crunched on the gravel path leading away from the landing area, the sense of quiet growing as I moved. The path soon gave way to open land, leading me to a small circle of standing stones. They were rough-hewn guardians of memory, encircling nothing but air.

I circled the stones, my fingertips grazing their weathered surfaces. Salt-laden air filled my lungs, and the crash of waves nearby played a rhythmic counterpoint to my heartbeat. Here, where grass bowed under the sea spray's kiss, a crust of salt clung to the blades like frost.

"Feels like standing in a different world." The ocean stretched into eternity. For a moment, a flight of unlimited imagination, I imagined what it would be like to let go, to be as untamed and unrestrained as the wind tangling through my hair and the waves crashing into the cliffs nearby.

Free as an elf.

Next to me the air shimmered, a ripple across my vision like heat on pavement. I blinked, but the distortion grew, coalescing into a form. Slender, raggedy edged, with long black hair that seemed somehow both tangled and perfect at the same time.

"Hello, Cassie," the person said, their voice sweet, perfect, and inhuman as a wind chime.

"Who are you?" I took a step back.

"Dream." The pseudo teenager before me smiled, a knowing curve to her lips. Her skin was dead white, with no color to it but a slash of red on her lips, and her eyes, the same color as the sea with no whites or pupils, were fixed on me.

Unnerving didn't begin to describe her.

Dream. I'd heard of this entity. Martellus spoke about Dream's awakening when we returned from that dimension.

Bran, solemn as ever, shook his head. "A terrifying change, but worth the risk." His distant gaze reminded me and Roma just how old he was, with many memories he didn't speak of.

"Would you leave this place, Cassie? Abandon the mortal realm to learn of your magic?" Dream's question meant she'd heard my thoughts.

"Why are you asking me?" I asked, curiosity warring with caution.

"Shay dreams of you, worries for you," Dream said, those eyes shifting to reflect the racing gray clouds in the sky. "I have seen and heard my son's mate's concerns. I wish to assist you."

"Assist?" I wrapped my arms around myself, feeling the weight of Shay's hidden fears. My friend had so many.

I paused, the strangeness of discussing such an offer with the embodiment of a concept not lost on me. "I can take care of myself, Dream. But... maybe learning wouldn't be so bad. Your realm is beautiful, I've only seen a tiny scrap of it."

"Correct." Dream nodded once, her smile widening. Her teeth were sharp and as white as her skin. "My invitation stands, whenever you're ready to accept it."

My attention snapped away from Dream as Aiden's familiar form materialized from a mist that hadn't been there a second ago. He stepped forward, his movements betraying a politeness that seemed to layer steel hard tension.

Worry radiated off him like heat from sun-warmed stone.

"Respect, Dream." He bowed his head ever so slightly in a gesture that spoke more of concern than deference.

"Congratulations, Aiden," Dream acknowledged with an impish grin, her attention shifting between us. "Your majesty. I see you're invested in Cassie's decision."

Sweet and pure, her voice was scary beyond reason.

Aiden's jaw tightened, and it was clear to me that Dream's focus on me had struck a chord in him, one that didn't resonate with harmony. The waves behind us chose that moment to crash against the cliff, sending a spray of salty droplets that clung to our skin.

"Indeed, Dream," Aiden said. "Your interest is noted. As is your ability to manifest on Earth again."

She laughed, like silver bells in the underworld.

The scene was too surreal not to find humor in it. Dream caught my expression and her hand swept through the air. She gathered a handful of salt-water out of thin air, as if plucking a ripe fruit from an invisible tree.

"Next time we meet." Dream flicked the gathered water at Aiden, "I'll come in a form grander than this." Her chiming words were light, teasing, yet they carried a weight that made Aiden stiffen. "Perhaps a figure taller, stronger, and more dashing than even the elf king here."

"Is that so?" I asked, shaking my head at the absurdity. Aiden, for all his composed exterior, couldn't quite hide a flicker of annoyance as he shook his head, flicking off the droplets trickling down his face.

"Until then," Dream finished with a flourish, leaving the lingering promise of a return hanging in the air as she faded from view.

Aiden exhaled slowly. “Shall we seek the castle?"

Aiden’s steps were silent as he and I walked up the path leading to the castle. The air closer to the building was thick with the smell of rain on ancient stone.

More rain spit on us.

"A word of caution about Dream." Aiden glanced sideways at me with those vivid eyes of his. "They are not of our world, and their kindness... even well intended, might not end up being as they hope."

"How so?" My curiosity was piqued, but I kept my eyes fixed ahead. Shay's castle was an imposing sight, a merciless pile of stone against the darkening skies.

"Let's just say Dream's realm operates under different rules. What seems benign can be a snare." Aiden's words held a seriousness that made me pause.

"Thanks for the heads-up." I meant it, though the idea of anything being more dangerous than my own recent experiences felt hard to believe.

We continued in silence until the castle itself loomed directly over us. Its massive gray stones rose high, ivy creeping like veins across its surface. Crenelated battlements cut into the sky, interrupting my view of the scudding clouds. Old merged with new in places. Glass windows reflected the stormy clouds, a testament to Shay's effort to drag the place into the present without sacrificing its soul.

"Geez," I said, feeling dwarfed.

Aiden surveyed it with a hint of disdain. "A bit underwhelming, isn't it?"

"More like intimidating." The heavy wooden doors we approached looked like they could withstand a siege.

"Intimidation could be a form of protection, I guess." He pushed one of the doors open with ease that belied its size. "After you."

I stepped into the grand entrance, centuries closing around me.

"Good, let me show you to your rooms so you can freshen up before you eat," said Butler.

"I'll be back in the morning," Aiden said. "Be well, Cassie."

I followed Butler into the castle. His steps echoed in the vast hall as he led me up a narrow spiral staircase. The stone walls were cold, almost chilling to the touch, but the flicker of LED-lit torches in iron sconces bathed everything in a warm glow. It was like stepping into another time, yet I could hear the faint hum of modern heating beneath the echoes.

"Your room is just up here, Miss Quinn," Butler said encouragingly.

"Thank you," I said. Each step was worn down from centuries of use, and I wondered how many feet had climbed them before mine.

We reached the top, and he gestured toward a heavy wooden door with a wrought-iron handle. "Let me know if there's anything needed for your comfort. The evening meal will be ready in an hour."

The door creaked open to reveal a spacious bedchamber. A canopy bed with dark wooden carved posts dominated the center, draped in rich blue and green fabrics. Across from it, a stone fireplace large enough to walk into promised warmth, though its fire was electric, dancing behind glass.

A guitar rested in a display case, with several books on a stand next to it.

"Wow," slipped from my lips before I could stop it.

"Is it to your liking?" Butler asked, a hint of pride in his tone.

"Very much so," I said. It was like something out of a fairy tale, if fairy tales came with discreet power outlets and a WIFI router on an antique writing desk.

"Your bathroom is through there." He pointed to another door.

"Thanks. I need that right now." I thought about the turmoil of the day.

"Of course. If you require anything else, please don't hesitate to call." With a nod, he left, closing the door softly behind him.

I approached the bathroom. The door opened to a sleek, modern space that contrasted sharply with the bedroom. Chrome fixtures gleamed against marble tiles, and a glass shower stall stood ready with fluffy towels stacked nearby.

After peeling off my travel-weary clothes, I stepped into the shower. Hot water cascaded over me, soothing too tight muscles and aches from riding a horse. I'd heard it hurt, and that was correct. The steaming spray felt wonderful, and I closed my eyes, letting the warmth envelop me.

"Okay, Cassie," I said to myself. "You can handle this. You've handled worse."

Water flowing over me, jets soothing tired muscles, my shoulders relaxed as I breathed in the scented air.

Wrapping the towel tightly around me, I stepped out of the bathroom, steam trailing in my wake. The luxurious bed whispered an invitation to sleep, even though I should go to eat.

Just as I began to comb through my damp hair, my phone buzzed on the nightstand. Roma's name flashed on the screen.

"Hey." I braced myself for whatever might come next.

"Cassie, do you think you can handle being around alchemists right now?" Roma's voice was firm yet tinged with concern.

"Uhm, why?" I asked, puzzled, my hand pausing mid-stroke. I'd stiffened. Franklin had been a member of the alchemist's organization, and they had siphoned Roma's magic from her.

"There's talk about using the wedding as neutral territory for the Council and the alchemists to meet. But I know your history with them," she said carefully.

Emotions flickered through me, dark and bitter, but I pushed them aside. "I can deal with it. What do you need from me?"

"Great. I'll send you the contacts for the invitations. You settled? Doing okay?"

"Always am," I said, though we both knew that wasn't entirely true.

I laid the phone back down on the nightstand.

A knock at the door startled me, and I hastily grabbed a robe, cinching it around me as I walked over to open it.

Aiden stood there, an unreadable expression on his face.

How on earth had he found my room?

He held out something that caught the light, sending sparkles dancing across the walls.

"Thought you might like this." He revealed a necklace of finely worked silver and gold with glittering blue-white stones so large they bordered on absurd. It was beautiful in a gaudy, fantastical way.

"Wow, Aiden, it's... something." I couldn't help but smile. "These can't be real."

He only grinned in response, and I wondered briefly if perhaps, in his world, they could be. No, that was silly. I took the necklace, the cool weight of it surprising against my skin.

"Thank you," I said, still somewhat bemused by the extravagance of the gesture. "It's certainly a statement piece."

"Only the best for you," Aiden said, a twinkle in his eyes that suggested he was in on some joke I hadn't quite caught onto yet.

"May I?" Aiden asked, gesturing toward the corner of the room where the old guitar rested on a stand.

"Sure," I nodded, still holding the necklace. Its faux

gems caught the fading light as I settled onto the edge of the bed robe tucked around me.

It covered as much as any clothing I wore, more than some.

Curiosity piqued, I watched him claim the instrument, his fingers gliding over it with assurance before he took a seat across from me.

Aiden strummed a chord, his hands sure and deft.

"I composed this for you," he said softly, intimately. The blue depths of his eyes held mine, intense and unguarded.

As the first notes rolled over me, a melody unfurled like a silken ribbon of emotion. Each note found a hidden place within me, echoing through the chambers of my heart. Opening the door, I'd locked and barred as my marriage crumbled. His tune, complex and haunting, was mostly in minor keys. Its unexpected turns tugged at something deep inside me.

It pulled me on a journey through the shifting realms of joy and sorrow, hope and longing.

"Whoa," I said as the last echo faded. "That was... I've never heard anything like it."

I leaned forward, drawn by the lingering notes of the melody and the desire on Aiden's face. My hand reached out, brushing against his where it rested on the guitar. The warmth from his skin beckoned me closer.

If the music echoed how he saw me...he thought I was beautiful, desirable. I closed the distance between us.

Our lips met, and a shiver ran through me. His lips parted under mine, and his gentle invasion of my mouth ignited a surge of something wild and untamed in me. The kiss remained gentle, a contrast to the storm of feelings that raged within, and I allowed myself to melt into the sensation.

As quickly as the spark had ignited, reality crashed into me. I pulled back, my breath catching in my throat.

"I shouldn't have—" Heat rose in my cheeks.

Aiden put a finger on my lips in a caress, a smile playing on his lips. "You don't need to apologize. Unless you want to do so by kissing me again."

My heart raced, conflicting emotions spinning through me. Relief was dominant when he didn't move any closer, respecting the space I'd instinctively put between us. I wanted him too much, too soon, and I was grateful he didn't push me.

"Maybe later." I glanced away from his face. A large part of me that wanted more kisses, but scars from the past burned me, reminding me to tread carefully.

He stroked my cheek, then settled the guitar and walked to the door, leaving me alone with my confusion.

7
AIDEN

I COULD FEEL the twin heat of jealousy and worry simmering beneath my skin, an alien and unsettling sensation. Another, softer and even more strange emotion was lodged near my breastbone where I had no wish to examine it.

Dream had been lingering around Cassie, his presence an unwanted threat and lure in this place. The emotions brought another into startling clarity that startled, that I desired Cassie, and more than desired, perhaps, and the thought of Dream wooing her twisted my insides into a silent snarl.

"Vent outside," I said, barely a whisper as I tore myself away from the doorway of Cassie's bedroom. The air outside was brisk, a sharp contrast to the warmth I'd left behind. My steps were quick, decisive as I strode toward the edge of the island, where land met void. With a whistle that cut through the silence, I called for my horse.

Cu descended gracefully from the sky, an ethereal silhouette against the moonlit night. I mounted in one fluid motion, and together we soared upwards, leaving behind the world of man and its tangled emotions. Knew where the other elves gathered and Cu flew at full speed, so only moments later the volcano loomed ahead.

Red painted its face, a steaming cauldron with its belly full of fire and brimstone. Magma streaked the air as the eruption continued.

Hovering above, I found Matilda and some others, almost a full band, lounging amidst the chaos of the eruption. The magma's glowing yet dim light cast their sharp features in a glow a mortal might find mesmerizing and terrifying.

It meant they were bored and giving them a task was wise if I didn't want Cassie hopping around in real fury.

And I had a task, fueled by anger that had been simmering long enough.

"Find me this Franklin, possessed by Formless Ones, hunted by the Goblins and shifters." I locked eyes with my sister. "He's a worm of a man, slippery and deceitful. Bring him to me alive but ensure he's no longer... capable of causing nuisances."

She nodded once, the gleam of the hunt on her face, making her features almost sharp enough to cut. The song of the hunt was in all our blood, and this presented both competition and challenge.

The smile that passed from face to face and the gleam of lust that followed- not physical lust, but for the emotions of the hunt- would have unnerved Cassie.

They'd be sated when this Franklin was brought to me and would not alarm any humans present.

They dispersed into the air, a flight of hawks seeking their prey. Franklin would soon be facing a reckoning, and it would hurt him as much as he'd harmed the woman who'd caught my interest. Turning my steed back toward the island, I knew the next measure of this dance awaited me, with Cassie, amidst the dawn and the breakfast table.

I hoped it was not to be the green fruit on toast so beloved.

Circling back to Fellmere Island, my mind remained a whirlwind of conflicting emotions. The cool night air soothed some of the frustration simmering within me, while I examined events.

Cassie had not liked the necklace, the one I'd meticulously created, believing the diamonds enhanced the depth of her hazel eyes.

"Why did she not like the gift?" I said to myself, dismounting at the edge of the cliff where the waves smashed against rock.

The memory of her laugh, light and unimpressed, puzzled me. I'd expected... what? Pleasure in its beauty, perhaps.

Or some sign that she saw me not just as a bystander or a problem to deal with but as someone worthy of memory and thought. Someone who wanted to gift her with adornment that matched her own natural brilliance.

"A song instead of a jewel. And I'll ask for a kiss, let her know how much I welcome it." The thought lightened my mind, fitting both my instincts and hers. It was a fair trade, my efforts for the soft press of her lips.

That fleeting moment held the promise of so much more. Her kiss. By the stars, her kiss. It lingered on my lips like the aftertaste of finest mead, intense, heady, intoxicating. A reckless spark springing from the storm inside her, and I wanted to taste her flame. To feel her breath mingling with mine, our boundaries blurred into nothingness...

"I'd forgotten how alluring humans could be." I spoke to the darkness, half-hoping the night would swallow my words, half-wishing they'd reach her ears. "She could make a man forget his own name."

I enjoyed the memory of her leaning into me once more, her vulnerability shielded by a fire that dared me to come closer. She's been harmed, and so hesitated and drew a boundary, one that she wasn't yet ready to cross. I respected that. I'd wait, as long as it took, for her to invite me over that threshold.

The fruit would be sweeter for waiting for it to

ripen. Though one could perhaps hasten the process a bit...

Kisses could become the currency for favors, in addition to the pure entertainment of watching her.

As I watched, the first tendrils of dawn began to streak the sky. The slow unfolding of its beauty reminded me to be patient, to savor each moment shared, to woo this woman who had unwittingly ensnared my interest.

I found Cassie at the breakfast table, her focus on the array of food before her, including the nasty green fruit on toast. She didn't notice my approach, so I cleared my throat to announce myself.

"Good morning." I filled a plate with eggs and ham. "Do you still desire help with the wedding plans?"

She glanced up, a spark in her hazel eyes, then laughed, a clear, unguarded sound. "Sure." She said, pushed a stray lock of her wavy black hair behind her ear. "Are you offering to help with all the planning?"

"Could be fun," I said.

"For some definitions of the word fun." Cassie stood up, gesturing for me to follow. "Let's see what we're working with for the venue."

We walked through the castle, the great hall standing proud in its preserved medieval glory, the open space echoing with memories. When we ascended the stairs, the upper rooms revealed a different story. Modern luxuries woven seamlessly into the old stone.

"Butler mentioned tents would be needed for more than ten guests." Cassie peered out of a window fitted with new glass.

"Tents would work." I'd spent time in any number of them.

"Yeah, I'm not thrilled about it," she said. "Given the people coming, there will be squawking about it, especially depending on who gets the inside rooms. Do you think we could just ferry people from other islands or the mainland?"

"Turning this place into a campground will be difficult," I said. At the very least, they'd need to dig a trench for bathroom use. "Given the weather, I don't think ferries would be viable, but I'll look into it."

"Thanks," Cassie said with a warm smile at me. "I need the help."

"Glad to be of service." I reached for her hand. She blinked as I raised it to my lips.

Then she blushed and stepped closer to the window.

I rubbed the back of my neck, trying to imagine what humans found appropriate to these festivities. "So, what else do you need aid with? Invitations, flowers...?"

Cassie glanced back at me, her hazel eyes full of amusement and patience. "Invitations, yes. Also, food for the reception, a special cake, music, planning seating arrangements..."

"Seating arrangements?" I said. Why wouldn't they simply sit according to rank?

"Trust me, it's like a strategic battle plan," she said with a wry grin.

"As you wish." I shifted my weight, trying to imagine where I could fit into all this. "What about... isn't it a custom to the bride after the ceremony? I've heard of that tradition. My friends would love to help kidnap her, and the goblins could try to defend her."

Cassie looked horrified for an instant, then laughed, the sound bouncing off the stone walls. "No, Aiden, that's not a part of modern weddings."

"Ah," I said, a tinge of disappointment cooling my enthusiasm. "Just thought it might add some excitement."

Cassie's laughter faded into a thoughtful pause, and she turned her attention toward the window. The sunlight painted her profile in warm hues as she regarded the glass and the view.

"There's another tradition that's much safer but just as important, the wedding dance."

"Wedding dance?" I said, intrigued. I liked the idea of a chance to dance with Cassie.

"I had a friend, she had this beautiful waltz at her wedding..." Cassie drifted off, smiling dreamily at the memory.

"Show me." I stepped closer to her. The idea of learning a new human dance, especially from Cassie, appealed to me.

"You'll have to follow my lead." She chuckled, clasping her hands together as if she could barely contain her excitement.

"Lead the way," I said, confident in my ability to pick up whatever steps she threw at me. "What is the music it's danced to?"

Cassie hummed a few bars, her voice sweet but soft, setting the tempo. I closed my eyes, letting the rhythm sink in before I mimicked it.

"Like this?" I hummed back after her, matching her beat for beat.

"Exactly like that." Cassie clapped her hands together and stepped into position, taking my hand in hers and placing my other hand on her waist.

"Ready?" she asked.

"Always," I said. Then I continued humming, feeling the pull of the music.

We moved as one entity, Cassie guiding me through the steps with a gentle nudge of her hand, her body close to mine. Each turn and step we took felt charged with an energy, filling the empty spaces of the hall with echoes of desire.

"See? No need for kidnapping when you can have this," Cassie said breathlessly, her laughter mingling with the notes we hummed. "Exciting, right?"

"Oh yes," I said. The simple act of dancing with her was most pleasurable.

Cassie blushed. "Stick with me and I'll show you just how exciting a dance can be."

We slowed, and Cassie's body eased against mine, her breath warm on my neck. Her green flecked eyes lifted to mine, wide and shimmering with something that looked a lot like desire. A dreamy smile played on her lips, and I leaned down and captured that smile with my own.

"Is this part of most wedding traditions too?" I said between soft presses of lips.

"Could be for the wedding night," she whispered back, her fingers tracing patterns on the back of my hand, setting off a thrill of pleasure wherever they touched.

I pulled her closer, our bodies fitting together as if we were two halves of the same whole. One of her hands slid up to tangle in my hair, while the other remained anchored at my waist, holding me close. The kiss deepened, and there was a moment where everything else fell away – just Cassie and me and the heat building between us.

Deepening the kiss, I slid my hands down to her rounded hips, pressing her into me. She shivered and arched her back, and I broke the kiss to nibble along the line of her jaw. She moaned, and emboldened, I slid a hand up to her ribs, just below her breast.

She stiffened in my arms, her hand pressing against my chest. "Stop," she gasped, her voice barely audible. "It's too soon."

I let her go reluctantly, scanning her face, searching for any sign of what had triggered her fear. Her cheeks were flushed, lips swollen, eyes still dark with desire. She held herself stiff, wrapping her arms around herself.

She needed space. No good huntsman would press her now.

"Of course." I stepped back further. "I'll tend to other matters for an hour, then return."

She nodded.

"I owe you for that kiss. Remember, we elves pay our debts" The playfulness in my tone hid the sincerity behind my words.

I winked at her, and she rolled her eyes, relaxing her stance.

After taking one last look at her, I turned and strode away, already plotting how to repay the debt in a way that would leave us both wanting more.

8
CASSIE

The low hum of conversation buzzed through the speakerphone, punctuated by the intermittent clink of silverware on ceramic as I picked at the remains of my meal.

Rain splashed against the windows, followed by a blast of wind. The WIFI wasn't up to any kind of images, so while the rest had video, I was listening in.

"Hey." Shay's quiet voice came on the line, instantly silencing the chatter. Her tone carried a weight, a significance that had me pausing to listen closely.

"What's up?" Cathy asked.

I could almost see Shay's usual nervous tic, the way she'd twine a golden strand around her finger when something big was on her mind.

"I've got news," she said.

"Hit us with it," Rey said.

A long pause, then Shay exhaled audibly. "Martellus and I... we're getting married."

A momentary silence engulfed the call, a swelling pause before an eruption of congratulations that would ensue. I glanced toward the window, the gray afternoon light making the room murky, thinking of Shay and Martellus, two guarded hearts finding solace in each other.

A like in the dimness. I was happy Shay had found the resolve to commit.

"Congratulations," Roma boomed through the speaker, aggressive and excited. "That's amazing. You could get married at the same time as me. It would be epic."

Also, knowing her, she was making sure Shay didn't back out due to second guessing herself.

There was a brief silence on the line, everyone taking a moment to process Roma's proposition. Including me. That wouldn't add anything to the planning, oh no.

It took Shay a moment to compose her response, and when she did speak, her words were measured and deliberate.

"I don't want a big ceremony." Shay spoke quietly, yet firmly enough to carry over the buzz of enthusiasm.

I leaned forward, clasping my hands together as if to gather everyone's focus through the phone. "No, hang on." I tried to sound as convincing as possible. "This would be the best idea ever because we would all be together at the same time."

There was a shuffle on the line, probably Shay's fingers tapping as she considered the proposition. I imagined Shay standing in her house, away from prying eyes, dreading the thought of being the center of such fanfare.

Martellus on the other hand...I didn't know him well, but I thought he'd relish the chance to have everyone see that Shay had taken him for a husband.

"Okay," Shay said, her tone suggesting a compromise in the making. "But I want it to be clear. I want a small, private ceremony. It can be before or after the big blowout wedding that Roma and Bran need to have."

Her chosen words came out with a precision that left no room for argument, yet the intent was gentle. It was classic Shay, allowing herself to be swayed but still holding on to what mattered most to her.

Her wedding would be a moment for just her and Martellus, intimate and quiet, before the grandeur demanded for Roma's event. I smiled to myself. Shay always knew how to navigate through the chaos with grace.

"Wait, back up," Roma cut through the chatter with a sharp edge. "This has become a blowout wedding?" There was the familiar clink of something, probably her overworked coffee mug, hitting the table.

"Yes, my love," Bran said, solemn as ever and tinged with that dignified patience he seemed to have in endless supply. "You're not just marrying me, you're becoming Queen of the Goblins, and of Dream." He paused, and I could picture his long white hair shimmering as he inclined his head, even though I couldn't see him on the group call. "Though we'll avoid mentioning the latter too loudly, considering Dream is awake again."

"Still." Roma huffed. “It’s a wedding, not a stunt."

"Speaking of stunts," Cathy said, serious for once. "Roma and I think she should invite the alchemists and the Council to her wedding. It might help prevent war."

"I agree," Shay said softly.

"Franklin's playing with fire," Cathy said, and my heart rate picked up at the mention of my ex-husband. "We got a taste of what's coming with the Formless Ones when those fake customs officials nabbed us. People need to unite to drive them off, and nothing like a wedding to provide neutral ground for people to talk."

A collective hum of thought resounded before there was silence, her words sinking in.

"Then it's settled," Roma said after a moment. "We need all the allies we can get. If Franklin's involved..."

"We've got the MIIB on board," Bran said. "They've offered security for the event, along with the various allies amongst the races of Dream."

"Good," Roma said. "That's one less thing to worry about."

I glanced out of the window, the soft light filtering through the glass. The idea of such threats lurking in the shadows sent a shiver down my spine. If only everything could be as tranquil and simple as the view outside. Then, life had never really given us that luxury, had it?

"Hey, Cassie," Roma said. "Could you reach out to Aiden and see if he's willing to share information? Bran says the Elves have intel on the Formless Ones we don't."

I was glad there was no video as I blushed. Leaning back in my chair, my fingers tapped over the table's surface. "Sure, I can talk to him."

Why Bran thought Aiden might be holding back information, I didn't need to ask. Many things in the supernatural world were guarded tighter than a dragon's hoard.

"Thanks, we could use all the help we can get," she said.

The call ended with a flurry of goodbyes and promises to update each other. Alone again, I let out a long breath, the silence of the room pressing down on me. My mind drifted to Aiden – who would be back soon. Whose presence made my heart race.

Was I ready for more? Franklin's shadow loomed large over any thoughts of intimacy. His betrayal had carved deep, jagged scars into my heart, ones that flared painfully at the worst moments. Yet with Aiden, it was different. I wasn't sure if it was the elf attitude toward freedom, because it certainly wasn't a completely positive thing, or if it was just the kind of man he was. He made me feel desired, but he had no wish to own me.

Maybe, just maybe, I was ready to consider moving forward. Not just for the sake of companionship but because Aiden, unlike Franklin, would never take more than I chose to give.

Also, it would quiet my horde of matchmaking friends.

I pushed the door open, stepping out into the humid air. It had finally stopped raining.

The vast expanse of sky and sea here was worth the trip. I inhaled deeply, cleansing the clutter of anxiety that kept trying to set up housekeeping in my brain.

I wandered along the path that crossed the island, lost in the sound of seabirds and the crash of waves. The landscape's beauty was stark, rock and earth and sea.

"Never thought I'd get used to the lack of green." The corners of my mouth lifted ever so slightly.

"Rather monotonous, isn't it?" The words were cawed from above. My head snapped up; a raven perched on a low branch. It regarded me, with silver and green eyes like Dream's.

"Could do with a bit more variety." I played along.

"Variety is the spice of life, true," came another voice, familiar and warm. Aiden walked around the bend in the path, hands tucked casually into his pockets. "Over seasoning can make a meal inedible. Speaking of which, Dream here seems to have taken a liking to conversation over solitary brooding."

"Brooding is boring," Dream squawked, fluttering his dark wings.

A wary smile tugged at my lips as I watched them, elf and the raven, trying to be casual about eyeing each other for weak points. "Are you planning on declaring a truce?"

"Something like that," Aiden said with a shrug. "We're working together on a project to please someone we both like. Or at least trying to."

"Good luck with that," I said. Working and playing well with others was not an elven trait, as I'd seen during the past several months.

"Thanks." He flashed a hundred-watt smile. "We need it."

"We've been busy with a little project in Alfheim," the raven cawed, bobbing its head approvingly.

"Really?" I was curious despite myself. "What kind of project?"

"Let's just say it's a gift for you and your guests." Aiden's slow smile and warm gaze suggested a secret he was itching to share. "Would you care to see it?"

"Sure." My heart skipped a beat at the expression and attention focused on me. "Lead the way."

We hurried toward the castle's edge where a portal shimmered like a mirage against the stone walls. Stepping through felt like plunging into cool water, the sensation brief but jarring. When we emerged on the other side, the landscape took my breath away.

"Wow," was all I managed as I took in the rustic lodgings before us.

"Your guests will be staying here." Aiden watched my reaction closely. "Each cabin has its own unique view."

The cabins were beautiful, constructed from rough-hewn wood and stone that seemed to grow organically from the ground. No two faced the same direction, yet each offered a frame to the stunning vistas beyond: rolling hills, dense forests, and rivers that caught the sunlight like veins of gold.

"Those beds," I pointed to a four-poster visible through an open doorway, "they look straight out of a magazine shoot."

"Ah, you caught me," Aiden said with a chuckle. "Dream and I might have borrowed the idea from a magazine photo you lingered on."

I nodded, impressed. "You both did a great job." I meant every word. They had managed to capture a sense of luxury and comfort that would make anyone feel at home.

I lingered at the threshold of a cabin, biting my lip. "It's beautiful," I said again, but a frown creased my forehead. The practical part of me skirmished with the unexpected offer.

Though I wasn't entirely sure my guests would accept this. Before trusting the king of elves and Dream, they might prefer tents. We would see. I wasn't going to turn this gift down.

"Then it's settled." Aiden spoke gently, as if he

sensed the battle raging within me. "They'll stay here."

"Okay." The word came out soft, almost lost in the rush of wind through the trees.

His smile held relief and something warmer, more intimate. He took a step closer, his hand lifting to capture mine. His lips brushed the back of my hand so lightly it might have been a leaf falling. My breath hitched, warmth spreading up my arm.

"Thank you," he said, his gaze not leaving mine.

"For what?" The fluttering in my stomach intensified, and I struggled to keep my tone even.

"For trusting me," he said simply.

Before I could respond, he opened his palm, revealing a delicate silver rose, its petals intricately wrought as if by magic. "This is from Alfheim," he said softly. "Your beauty shames it, but you deserve adornment worthy of your spirit."

I couldn't help the smile that broke through my reservations, nor the blush that warmed my cheeks. "It's stunning." I traced the soft petals. "Thank you."

Dream's laughter cut through the moment, a sharp yet playful caw breaking the moment.

Aiden and I turned toward the sound. The raven perched on a branch overhead, its beady eyes fixed on us.

"Perhaps," the bird's beak never moved though I could hear the words clearly, "you should allow me to take you to Dream, Cassie."

I frowned, a little worried by the insistence. "To Dream?"

"Indeed. Where else but in Dream can a mere mortal be outfitted as a true queen? The fabrics alone..."

The words trailed off into a series of amused clicks and ruffles of feathers as Aiden glared at the bird.

"Outfit me as a queen? Why?" If this was Dream's plan, I needed to nip it in the bud. Roma and Shay would be the stars of the day.

Or had Dream already offered them gowns as well?

"Absolutely." Dream fluffed its coal black feathers, making it appear larger, more imposing. "You'll dazzle them all, I assure you."

With that, the raven spread its wings wide and took to the sky leaving me wondering and worrying.

Aiden watched the bird ascend, a wry smile playing on his lips. "Dream enjoys their theatrics."

"So, I've heard," I said, still staring at the space where the raven had been. The idea of being dressed by Dream intrigued me, but I couldn't shake off the feeling of someone trying to make me a pawn in a game. I'd had that experience and still had the emotional scars.

9
CASSIE

I LEANED back in the wooden chair, spine popping as a sigh escaped me. Two weeks of non-stop prep had left its mark – my eyelids were heavy, but there the content of completed work filled me. With still more to be done, true, but much was complete.

Today, I had two chefs to interview in person and a florist to choose via a video call. The thought alone made my spine straighten a bit.

"Busy day ahead," I said. I couldn't keep relying on Aiden for lifts, so I'd be taking the helicopter.

My days had melded into a pattern: read a chapter, organize a part of the wedding, listen to a song, repeat. Franklin's shadow cleared a bit with each passing day, my mind warming and rejuvenating like tilled earth under the morning sun.

Music helped. I'd sway alone to the tunes, pretending not to wish Aiden was dancing with me.

The flirting – nothing too bold, just enough to feel a flutter now and then. Aiden's presence was a strange blend of comfort and excitement, something I hadn't anticipated.

"Florists and chefs, that's the agenda." The lingering thoughts of Aiden would have to wait. There was work to be done. First, getting breakfast.

I was pouring coffee when Aiden strolled in, a smear of dark ash across one perfect cheek, dusting his clothes. His blond hair somehow looked gorgeous despite the fact it looked like he'd combed it with firecrackers.

"Morning," I said flatly, pushing a mug toward him without a question. "Today is about food and flowers."

He poured himself coffee, the ash dusting from his sleeve falling like gray snowflakes onto the counter.

"Sounds festive," he said with a half-smile.

"Off to London to test out some chefs." I watched for a reaction.

His grin grew, blue eyes lighting up in that way that made my heart do somersaults. Without thinking, I stepped closer and planted a quick kiss on his lips, curious what he'd do this time.

Aiden responded with a light press of his own lips against mine, then lifted my hands to his mouth and kissed each in turn. "I'll see you there," he promised, leaving a trail of soot on my skin from his hands. "I'll bring some seasoning, too, so you can really test these cooks."

"London's a big place, Aiden," I said, but he just winked and walked away, leaving me to wonder exactly how he planned to find me.

The helicopter landed, and I gathered my bag, still mulling over Aiden's words. How he'd find me was beyond me. Then again, Aiden was full of surprises.

A taxi ride later I stepped into the private kitchen for the taste test, I arranged my notes and peered at the up-and-coming chefs bustling with anticipation. They were about to be thrown a curveball they couldn't have expected.

"Good afternoon," I greeted them, just as the door swung open once more. Aiden sauntered in, changed and no longer ashy, nonchalantly carrying several small containers filled with powdery substances in colors that didn't belong in any earthly spice rack.

"Thought I might add a little interest to the menu." He locked eyes with me as he put the counters on the table. "Exotic, but harmless, I assure you."

One chef raised an eyebrow, taking a cautious whiff of the contents. The other chef, emboldened or perhaps just reckless, shook a small amount of the powder into his palm and tasted it directly.

"Interesting..." he said, eyes distant.

Fine, I'd play along. "Let's see what you can whip up. Something simple, like... eggs?"

One chef sprang into action. In moments, the air filled with the scent of butter and eggs mingling with the unknown seasonings. The other shook his head and walked out.

Aiden leaned against the counter, watching them work with an amused glint in his eye. He caught me staring and flashed a smile.

"Trust me," he mouthed.

I could only hope that his confidence was well-placed.

"These seasonings." I gestured to the array of vibrant powders lined up beside the stovetop. "Would you consider using them in the wedding menu?"

Chef Francois Legrand, with his salt-and-pepper hair and keen blue eyes, paused and glanced toward the containers. His lips curled into an intrigued smile. "Ms. Quinn, they are unlike anything I have tasted before. Tell me, where do they hail from?"

"Alfheim," I whispered, conscious of how fantastical it sounded.

"Ah, Alfheim," he exclaimed, chuckling as if I'd shared an inside joke. The twinkle in his eye suggested that he wasn't entirely disbelieving. "Well, then, incorporating a touch of magic into your sister's special day could be quite the talking point."

"Magic indeed." I watched him deftly fold the seasoned eggs onto a plate.

"Let's ensure they're safe for everyone first," I said, more to myself than to him. I had no intention of a disastrous incident.

"Of course." Chef Legrand distributed samples for us to taste.

The flavors exploded on my tongue, a symphony of new and delightful tastes. Aiden watched, a shadow of concern flickering across his face until he saw my satisfied nod.

"Then it's decided," I said decisively. "Yes, we'll use them."

"Excellent. This will be an adventure." Francois's enthusiasm was infectious, and I found myself grinning back at him, feeling a rush of excitement.

"Thank you, Francois. I appreciate how much effort you're putting into this."

"Anything for your happiness, Ms. Quinn." He

winked, and I felt a warm flush spread across my cheeks.

Just then, Aiden's phone buzzed insistently. He glanced at the screen, his expression shifting from relaxed to annoyed in an instant. "I have to take this." He stepped away.

"Is everything okay?" I asked.

"Potential earthquake," he said tersely. "I need to go."

"Be safe," I called after him, but he was already out the door.

I spent the rest of the day wrapped in a whirlwind of decisions and discussions, none of which filled the sudden void left by Aiden's abrupt departure. The video call with potential florists only deepened my frustration. The floral arrangements offered were lackluster, failing to capture the beauty and excitement I'd wanted.

"Nothing is right," I said to the screen after ending the call.

With a defeated sigh, I turned off the lights and trudged to bed, unaccustomed loneliness creeping in like an unwelcome chill. I missed Aiden's easy presence.

Along that road lay danger. After a long hot shower, I closed my eyes, willing myself to sleep and whisk me away from thinking about anything.

It seemed only a minute later I woke to a knock, with hazy morning light filtered through the curtains. Aiden's rumpled form leaned against the doorframe, the door open.

"Good morning, Cassie," he said, bright and cheerful.

"Hey." I sat up in bed. "You look wide awake. Did you manage to get any sleep?"

"None," he said. "But I don't really need it, either. I had to deal with a... situation. It took some convincing to stop the earth from shaking."

"Shaking?" I said, puzzled.

"Some of my associates had grand ideas about redecorating parts of California and Washington state," he said with a hint of exasperation.

"Redecorating?" My concern gave way to curiosity. "How do you stop an earthquake?"

"Power, work, a fair bit of yelling at the people who set up the situation. Forget that for now." He straightened up, a smile playing on his lips. "If you're up for it, I have something to show you. Flowers."

How had he known about yesterday's flop?

"Really?" I sat up in bed, energized by the prospect. "I'd love to see them. Leave so I can dress"

"Great." He shut the door, and I pulled clothing on.

Minutes later, I found Aiden waiting with his horse, Cu, who looked beautiful with ribbons in his starlight mane. Aiden offered his hand, helping me mount behind him. Instinctively, my arms wrapped around his waist, holding on as we trotted away from the house.

We passed through an invisible barrier, the world around us blurring momentarily before snapping back into focus. The air felt different, charged with a familiar energy that tingled against my skin.

"We're going to Alfheim, aren't we?" I whispered, recognizing the sensation from before.

Aiden nodded, urging the horse forward. "Yes, to find the perfect blooms for your sister's wedding."

Cu slowed to a gentle trot, and the landscape opened into an expanse of wild beauty. My gaze swept across the field, where flowers of every imaginable color and kind bloomed in riotous abundance. I slid off the horse before Aiden could offer his hand, my feet sinking slightly into the soft earth.

"Wow," was all I managed, my eyes wide with wonder.

Aiden dismounted with ease. Cu blurred, then a silver dog stood in his place. He barked once, then flopped to the ground next to me. I took the hint and scratched his head. His tail thumped on the ground.

From the saddlebags now lying on the ground, Aiden pulled out a wicker basket, flashing me a grin. "I thought we might enjoy a small feast amidst the flowers."

"Picnic?" I raised an eyebrow. "Here?"

"Where better?" He gestured at the sea of blossoms

around us. "You can pick your favorites, and we'll celebrate your choices."

My heart fluttered at the thoughtfulness as he laid out a blanket and began unpacking the basket. There was bread, cheese, sliced fruits, and a bottle of wine nestled among ice packs. The aroma of fresh food mingled with the floral scent of the field, creating an intoxicating blend.

"Let's explore a bit, shall we?" Aiden offered his arm. "Then we can come back and eat."

"Lead the way." I slipped my hand through his arm as we wandered through the explosion of petals and scents. Somehow, each managed to be distinct without the entire aroma being unpleasant or overwhelming. Alfheim magic.

The further we walked, the more I realized how special this place was, each flower unique and more exquisite than the last. It felt like stepping into a painting, one where the artist had lavished attention on every brushstroke. The picnic waited for us, a promise of rest after our ramble through this enchanting corner of Alfheim.

Suddenly, the tranquil air split with a sharp cry. I jumped back as two figures burst through the underbrush, each clad in shimmering armor that caught the sunlight in dazzling patterns. They locked eyes with Aiden, their expressions full of fierce determination.

"King." Both bowed hastily, but with superhuman grace. "We seek your judgment."

Aiden's arm tensed beneath my hand, and he sighed, his gaze hardening as he regarded the duo. "Now is not the time, Caelum, Norian."

"Apologies, my lord," the one named Caelum said, his eyes darting toward me before quickly looking away. "The matter is urgent."

I could feel Aiden's annoyance radiating like heat from a flame. He stood taller, the playful light in his eyes replaced by a flare of anger.

"Very well," he said curtly, releasing my hand. "State your grievances."

The two elves exchanged a glance.

"Forgive us, your Majesty, for the inopportune time," Norian said, his voice suggesting he spoke for form's sake. A steely undertone suggesting this duel they spoke of wasn't something they would set aside easily.

I stepped back, giving Aiden space. His expression was a cold mask now, and I had a pang of loss for the peace of just moments ago.

Aiden turned to me, his voice even. "Cassie, do you mind if I settle this matter now? Or do you wish me to send them on their way to return at a time of our convenience?"

I hesitated, the sudden shift from our intimate escape to this formality jarring. "Yeah, go ahead."

My curiosity was piqued despite myself.

The two elves stepped away from Aiden and me, drawing their weapons with a grace that hid their intent. The air crackled with tension, an electric promise of violence.

"Begin," Aiden said, his tone leaving no room for argument.

The clash was swift, steel ringing against steel, as the elves moved with lethal precision. They were blurs of motion, their duel a dance of death. I flinched at flesh being torn, a grimace etching itself across my face.

Aiden stood by me, implacable as stone, eyes tracking each movement with clinical detachment. There was no hint of discomfort, no wince at the brutality unfolding before him.

The fight ended almost as quickly as it began, one elf standing victorious, the other crumpled on the ground. My stomach churned, the taste of bile rising.

It was one thing to know casual violence was a part of his world, another thing to see it in action.

"Enough," Aiden's voice interrupted the aftermath, and the victor sheathed his weapon with a respectful nod.

"Your judgment has been passed, my lord." He bowed slightly to Aiden.

"See to the wounded. I don't want him here right now," Aiden said, then turned back to me, his expression unreadable.

"Let's see more of the flowers," he said casually, as if

we'd merely witnessed a minor disagreement rather than a savage bout.

"Sure," I managed to say, my voice barely above a whisper, struggling to process the casual violence. I noticed the blood – dark and stark against the delicate petals of lovely flowers. My heart raced, remembering other fights, my head pounding.

Aiden followed my gaze, his brow furrowing before he waved a hand, murmuring words I couldn't catch. The blood vanished as if it had never been, but the image lingered, a shadow that no magic could erase.

"I think I want to go home now." My voice was steady, but inside, I felt anything but. There were too many emotions swirling within me, too much confusion.

"Of course." His tone was gentle, almost apologetic, and with another incantation, we were back on the island, away from the fields of Alfheim.

"I'm sorry it ended this way. I'll return with the dawn," he said to me as we crossed the threshold of the castle. Then he was gone.

That evening, in the quiet of my room, loneliness crept in on quiet feet like a cat looking for a treat. I sat at my computer, staring at the tenth change to the seating arrangements, my thoughts drifting. Aiden was attractive, yes, and there was an undeniable connection between us. We were worlds apart, literally. Could this light-hearted flirting lead to anything real? Did I want it to?

A lump formed in my throat. No tears, Cassie. You're stronger than this. Even damaged, you're healing.

I straightened my back, focused on the screen and began clicking and dragging names into different places. It was mundane work, but it took a lot of thought, the perfect distraction. Hours passed, blurring into a haze of names and table numbers until my eyelids grew heavy, and eventually, I slumped back.

The morning light woke me from fading dreams of silver roses. Groaning, I levered myself out of the chair and shuffled to the window, stretching.

A sweep of color across met my eyes, occupying an empty patch of earth where brown scrub and struggling grass had grown before. Flowers. Not just any flowers, but the exact ones I had admired most in Alfheim.

"Oh my." I pressed my fingers to the cool glass. Aiden had brought a piece of that magic here. For a fleeting second, warmth bloomed in my chest.

He cared. He was involved. As King, others of his people might follow in his footsteps. A flicker of concern followed the warmth in my breast.

I turned from the window. With many other elves involved, this wedding could turn into a spectacle of chaos. Defined boundaries were needed, rules.

Standing by the computer, I started typing a list. 'No talking food,' I wrote. 'No itchy dresses.' The more I considered the possibilities, the longer the list grew.

A lot of what I came up with would have made middle schoolers proud, but that was the level elf humor seemed to prefer.

"Payment," I said to myself. What could I offer Aiden for his help in enforcing these rules? It struck me: an invitation to the wedding and a favor he wouldn't refuse, a willing conversation with Bran. Guilt pinched at my conscience for using Bran as a bargaining chip but ensuring the wedding went smoothly was my priority.

"Sorry, Bran," I said, even though he wasn't there to hear my apology. "It's for the greater good."

I took a deep breath and continued typing. If this list kept the elves in line—yeah, right—I would avert impending madness.

I clicked 'send' and watched as the email vanished into the digital void, off to Bran with all its potential bargained promises.

Almost instantly, a ping sounded. Bran's reply popped up.

"If it keeps elvish jokes to a minimum, consider me enlisted," he wrote. I could hear the tone of voice he'd say it in with my head, dryly amused.

One less thing to worry about.

The door creaked open, breaking the silence of my makeshift office. Aiden sauntered in, then paused, frowning.

"You didn't rest well last night."

"True," I said, softer than intended. I reached for the jar on the desk, plucked out a piece of candy, a peace offering or maybe a bribe, and pushed it across the table toward him. While elves didn't need to eat, Aiden was very fond of sweets.

The sugar glinted under the room's lights, a small, bright red gem against the gleaming wood.

"Need your help." I met his gaze. "We've got to make a list. Your elves will need...guidelines for the wedding. Since I had a flash of intuition they plan to crash it."

I couldn't suppress the big eyes I made at him. The expression was absurd, but absurdity was my new normal.

Aiden's eyes sparkled as he took the candy, turning it over in his fingers. "A list of do nots, hmm?" He quirked a brow, curiosity piqued.

He wasn't denying the potential of wedding crashers either.

"Exactly," I said. "If anyone's going to turn the

bouquets into pythons or the champagne into pixie dust, it'd be them."

"It will be a long list," Aiden said, the corners of his mouth lifting in a half smile. "Requiring careful thought. Finding a way around it will become a hobby for some, so Leave a few harmless loopholes."

Aiden's lips brushed my cheek in a gentle kiss before he sat down opposite me.

"I'll owe you for this," I said.

"Yes," he said simply as the candy disappeared between his lips. He leaned back in his chair, a mischievous glint in his eyes. "Given the size of the task, I'd say a make-out session is not out of order as payment."

"Payment?" My eyebrows shot up in surprise. "Making out as a payment? Not what I had in mind."

Aiden reclined, resting his elbows on the back of the chair with casual poise. "Cassie," he said, a note of earnest inquiry lining his voice, "every time you've graced me with a kiss, I have offered a token in return. Is that not the custom among humans?"

I felt my face flush, indignation and humor swirling inside me. "No, Aiden." The words fell between a laugh and a scold. "When I give a kiss, it's given freely. No strings attached, no gifts necessary."

He looked puzzled as if the concept of unbartered affection was strange to him. “Why not do something you want to anyway as a payment?"

Was it really worth going over all the unfortunate human implications of his idea, or should I accept he was an elf and roll with it?

I considered the rogue gleam in Aiden's eyes.

Roll with it.

"All right." A rush of daring pulsed through me. "Let's get on with this 'make-out session' then. I’m still not considering it as paying for anything, but you can take it as you want."

He didn't need to be told twice. Rising from his chair, he closed the distance between us, a predator's grace in his every step. The air seemed to hum as he approached, and my heartbeat quickened. Crouching next to me, he cupped my face gently, his touch feather-light but sending ripples of heat cascading down my spine.

"Are you sure?" he asked, his voice a soft rumble.

"Absolutely," I said.

Our lips met, and it was nothing like the light, teasing kisses we'd shared before. This was a claiming, a melding of breath and desire that tore a gasp from my throat. Aiden's mouth moved over mine with a hunger that stoked the fire within me, his kiss deepening until the world narrowed down to the taste of him, the press of his body against mine.

His hands roved over my back, pulling me closer, leaving trails of searing warmth wherever they touched. My fingers tangled in his hair, tugging him nearer still, craving the intoxicating mix of tenderness and raw need he evoked in me. Our breaths mingled, ragged and urgent, as if we were drawing life from each other with each voracious kiss.

The room fell away, the list forgotten, as Aiden and I locked in an embrace that drove niggling unpleasant thoughts right out of my head. Nothing on weddings, or what needed to be done.

There was only the joy of being wanted, of me wanting in return, freely, fiercely, unshadowed by past hurts and expectations.

When we finally broke apart, chests heaving, faces flushed, Aiden tapped my nose. A silent agreement that whatever this was between us, it was worth exploring. It was worth the risk.

I moved my computer, and we sprawled across the couch, sheets of paper strewn around us like the aftermath of a snowstorm. Aiden's hand brushed mine as we both reached for the same pen, and his touch sparked a warmth that spread up my arm.

"Okay." I tried to focus. "New first item: do not enchant the food to talk or sing when bitten into." I scribbled it down, glancing at him to see if he grasped the gravity of the rule.

"Reasonable. Food often has no sense of pitch," Aiden said with a nod.

No, not going to ask.

"Next, no itchy clothing enchantments. That's just cruel."

"Agreed," he said. He leaned over to write it himself, his arm brushing against me, his proximity sending a shiver through my body.

I cleared my throat. "Keep the flower petals in the baskets normal. We don't need a mountain of petals following the flower girl down the aisle."

"Quite reasonable," he said, inches away now. His breath warmed my cheek, and I fought the urge to turn my face toward his.

"Also, absolutely no bouquets turning into snakes. That's horror movie material."

"Imagine the screams," Aiden chuckled softly before catching himself. "No snakes, then."

"God, this is gonna be a long list." I paused my hand mid-sentence.

Aiden looked at me, his gaze intense and sincere. "It will be as long as it needs to be, Cassie."

Our eyes locked. The pen dropped from my fingers as Aiden cupped my face gently, pulling me in for a deep kiss. His lips moved against mine with a tender urgency, conveying promises and desires without words.

As the kiss deepened, our hands roamed again, rekindling flame that had only been banked. His fingers traced the curve of my spine, sending tremors of longing coursing through me.

"Maybe," I whispered against his lips, "we should take a break from the list."

"Perhaps we should," Aiden said, his voice husky.

He picked me up, hurrying up the stairs to my room without needing to breathe heavily. Lean and strong, this elf.

In my bed next to me, he traced the lines of my face. With every gentle kiss we shared, I felt old wounds lessening, made less tender by trust and mutual desire.

"Beautiful," Aiden said. His touch was tender, and I nipped him.

"I'm not made of glass," I said.

As if he'd been waiting for the invitation, his kisses and touch became fiercer and more demanding, and I answered that demand. Hot and wild, as if he'd devour me whole, and I returned the favor, lingering on the beautiful lean length of him.

As he moved to settle between my legs, he paused.

"You're ready?" he asked, midnight blue eyes searching mine for any sign of discomfort.

"Yes. Move," I said.

Our movements took on a primal rhythm, the air charged with the electricity of our union. I clung to Aiden, my anchor in the maelstrom of sensation. Waves of pleasure crashed over me, and I cried out, and Aiden stiffened and joined me in my leap.

In the aftermath, as we lay entwined, I listened to the quiet thud of his heart. The world could wait.

I marched across the dew-covered grass to the small cluster of gathered elves, clutching the thick stack of papers to my chest. The list Aiden and I had composed had grown to ten pages, a detailed compilation of do's and don'ts, mostly don'ts, for the wedding. I carried multiple copies.

"Remember," I said as I came to a halt, "if you attend, you must promise by your name to abide by this list."

The elves gazed at me with curious and interested eyes, opposite of their solemn nods.

That expression meant trouble, I'd learned.

"Here." I handed over copies of the list.

Slender fingers flicked through it rapidly.

"Just so we're clear, not all of these rules are for the wedding day alone. Some are... let's say, more about general behavior in the human world." I crossed my fingers.

"Thou shalt not make all traffic lights green at the same time," Matilda read out loud, arching an eyebrow.

"Exactly," I said firmly. "Do you understand the importance of these guidelines?"

"After we've read it. I'll meet you again later today," said Matilda, glazing from face to face. The others nodded, and they retreated to their steeds.

I exhaled sharply as they left, feeling a strange mix of authority and anxiety. Who would've thought I'd be trying to integrate elves into the modern world?

Here's hoping there were no arguments. As I walked to the castle, I mulled over the list in my head. It was comprehensive, exhaustive even.

With the elves' proclivities, it felt necessary. If it helped prevent any problems at the wedding, it would be worth every hour putting it together.

10
AIDEN

I WATCHED THE EVENING UNFOLD, the rehearsal dinner buzzing with a strange energy.

"Humans and their strange ideas," I said under my breath, not fully grasping the need to practice festivities. Didn't they understand that nothing could be practiced enough to make it flawless if other beings were involved?

Cassie beamed like the moon in her joy, surrounded by her family and friends. Her happiness suspended my doubts. I'd do much to sustain that level of joy in her.

My human lover moved among the guests, her laughter filling the room. Her interaction fueled my momentary annoyances. It was a hard-won battle to not interfere with her socializing with them when every instinct screamed mine.

If they truly perceived the marvel she was, they'd try to steal her from me. That went double for my kindred. In point of fact, stealing human lovers was a time-honored game and tradition. One they had best not practice on Cassie. Being King now, I could be very pointed in my wrath if they tried it.

Besides, knowing her, she'd rescue herself and kick their butts bloody as she did so.

My gaze narrowed for just a moment when she reached Bran. He bowed slightly, his pale straight hair a contrast to her dark waves. She kissed his cheek, and he straightened up, a gentle smile curving his mouth. I gave him a hard look, since he was wedding her sister.

In my opinion he was getting the worse end of the deal, but he wanted Roma from all I'd been told. No accounting for taste.

As Cassie guided her companions through the stone corridors of the castle, her friend, the sibyl Shay, mentioned the mechanical innovations she'd had installed. The others listened with interest, but for me I wondered how the tedium could be borne.

What was radiant heat anyway?

I trailed the little group, my eyes scanning the area, not for appreciation, but precaution. The last thing we needed tonight was Shay to be triggered into prophecy.

It would cast a pall on events and make Cassie worried and sad.

"Is it just me or does Shay have the uncanny ability to make coin-counting sound like an epic saga?" I spoke softly to Martellus, who only grunted in response, his eyes fixed on Shay with love and worry.

As we moved down the hall, I remembered a decorative blade mounted above the hearth on a side hall, a few turns down. It had given off a vibe I didn't like when I first touched it, like it was waiting to be part of a story, one we didn't want told. Without a word, I excused myself and sprinted ahead of the group. My fingers wrapped around the hilt, and I felt that same odd shiver.

With a quick glance to ensure Shay could not see me or the blade, I pulled it from its ornamental prison and darted outside to the tower. Jamming it into the hidden slate rafters, I hoped it would be forgotten by time and fate alike.

I slipped back in, slightly damp from the light rain falling, but satisfied. No dark omen would fall upon our heads, and more importantly, Cassie was unperturbed, still smiling as she led the tour.

Later, as supper filled our bellies and conversation turned to the morrow's logistics, I leaned back in my chair, listening to their plans unfold.

So many ways they could go awry, I'd need to attend carefully to make sure they didn't so Cassie would be happy.

"Martellus, Hugh, and a few of the goblins will take care of escorting the guests through the portal to the guest houses," Cassie was saying, "We've decided not to tell them exactly where they are going."

"Rey's out then?" I asked, glancing at him sidelong. "Too much potential for trouble?"

"Exactly," Cassie said with a firm nod. I swallowed a laugh.

"Trouble? As opposed to what, elves?" Rey snorted, his eyes dancing with mockery as he met my gaze.

"Definitely 'yes' on that," Cassie said without missing a beat.

"Most of the guests are already tucked away in their rooms," I said casually, before turning to Shay with a mock-serious expression. "Shay, would you object much to your parents being eaten by dragons?"

They had been most irritating, trying to tell me I could become wealthy were I a model.

"Yes, Aiden," Shay said dryly, though her lips twitched in amusement. "They'd give the poor dragon indigestion."

Laughter echoed around the table, light and easy, but Martellus caught my eye, his silent gaze confirming that despite the jests, Shay's parents were off the menu. They needed to stay healthy and, more importantly, away from any real dragons.

Pity.

The meal wound down, and the clatter of cutlery faded into a comfortable hush. I rose to my feet and offered Cassie my arm, which she took with an ease that drew attention from Martellus and Bran.

There would be discussion behind closed doors this evening.

"Let's get you to your room." I guided her toward the grand staircase.

Since we were first to leave, the castle's corridors were silent, save for the soft patter of our steps on the stone floors. At her door, Cassie turned to face me, the warmth of her hands still lingering on my arm as she released it.

"Thank you," she said, her smile like a spotlight in the dimly lit hallway. Then, unexpectedly, she reached up on her toes and pressed her lips to mine, a kiss that held promises and whispered secrets.

"Will you come in?" Her voice was soft but confident.

"If you desire me to." My heart raced in anticipation.

Cassie's eyes danced with mirth and invitation. A glimpse of her I savored, knowing the shadows that often tried to claim her thoughts.

"I do," she said, her voice husky as she pushed the door open.

Inside her room, the air was scented with the light rose perfume she preferred. Pale moonlight spilled across the floor from the rare clear night, luminous, revealing and concealing. As Cassie closed the door behind us, sealing away the rest of the world, I was inspired.

First, it was important to arrange for good weather. Second, she'd have clothing that befit her for the wedding tomorrow.

"I'll have a gown for you," I found myself saying, "One as radiant as you are. It will shame the sun and humble the moon."

Her laughter filled the room, brighter than any star, and she shook her head, disbelief mingling with delight. "Aiden. It's fine. I have lots of clothes."

"Nothing good enough for you." I meant every word.

Then, drawn together by the force of our emotions, we sought each other's embrace. The night deepened around us, kind shadows and darkness for love's mysteries. For those hours, nothing else existed. Just Cassie and I, and the promise of a love between elf and human.

11
CASSIE

The morning sun hadn't yet chased away the remnants of a restless night from me when a knock sounded on the door to the room we'd made the communal dressing room for the wedding party.

I walked to the door and opened it a crack. Aiden, his arms cradling a garment as though it were a newborn, gave me a sheepish grin.

"Whoa," I stepped into the hall as he unfolded the dress for me. It was ethereal, all gauze and gemstones shimmering in the soft light, delicate yet stunning. The fabric seemed almost translucent but held a secret modesty, falling just right to complement my skin tone, casting a radiant sheen that would make me glow.

"Isn't it too much?" I asked, holding the dress against myself, suddenly self-conscious. "I mean, I can't be outshining Roma or Shay. You know, all bridesmaids are supposed to match."

Aiden cocked his head, considering. "Different colored dresses, I've seen it on your shows." He paused, then said, "Should I get gowns for Roma and Shay?"

"No, no." I considered the brides' fondness for their chosen attire. "They love their dresses. Let's not complicate things."

He nodded. “I'll be back in a moment."

The door latched softly behind me as I carried the dress in, and the room erupted into a racket of giggles and exclamations over the dress. We couldn't help ourselves, the situation was too absurd, too wonderfully bizarre. Cathy doubled over, clutching her stomach as she laughed, while Tanni's chuckles bounced off the walls, mingling with my own uncontrollable snickers.

"Who knew Elves had such... extravagant taste in fashion?" I managed to gasp out between fits of laughter.

At that moment, Martellus nudged the door open with his shoulder, his eyes clamped shut.

"Everything okay in here?" he asked, the corners of his mouth twitching as if he was fighting back his own amusement.

"Aiden." I wiped a tear from the corner of my eyes. "He just waltzed in here with a dress for me fit for a queen, not a bridesmaid."

"Ah, yes, well, dealing with Elves is always interesting," Martellus said, his deep voice resonating with resignation and exasperation. "They have a flair for the dramatic. If you have Aiden's full attention, try to get used to it, Cassie."

Just as the laughter in response to Martellus' comment started to subside, Aiden reappeared by him, his arms now filled with even more fabric, dresses for Cathy and Tanni. My jaw dropped.

I had picked out the bridesmaid dresses myself, and they were nothing like these. While beautiful, not something to wear to a wedding ceremony.

"Aiden," I smiled at him, trying to turn this into a silly game. "What's next? Are you going to bring me underwear too?"

He blinked twice, turned on his heel, and exited the room, clearly off to fulfill my request. The door hadn't even clicked shut before Roma snorted with laughter.

"Can't wait to see this Vegas number he brings back," Roma said.

"Girl, you know you asked for it," Tanni said, her voice trembling with laughter. "No getting mad, no matter how outrageous it looks."

I could only groan in response as the heat rose to my cheeks. Shay buried her face in her hands, shoulders shaking with mirth. "Oh my god, Cassie, what have you done?" she said, words muffled by her palms.

"Shay, your makeup," Cathy cried out just as Aiden swept back into the room, holding up an impossibly extravagant set of lingerie glittering with gemstones.

"Really?" I looked at the bra and panties, unsure whether I was on the verge of tears or about to collapse into hysterical laughter. "This doesn't exactly scream comfortable."

"Are those real diamonds?" Tanni whistled long and low, ogling the bejeweled, eyes dancing as she glanced at me.

"Absolutely. Comfortable too; I tried the bra myself," Aiden said with a grin that somehow managed to be both proud and sheepish.

"Magic, then." I tried not to imagine Aiden testing the fit of a bra. "Because we're definitely not the same size."

"Of course, it's magic," he said as if that cleared everything up.

"Thank you, Aiden." I ushered him toward the door again. "We need to get dressed now. While these dresses are beyond gorgeous, we can't wear something that competes with the brides."

"Wait, Cassie," Aiden paused, his expression hopeful. "What do you think about wearing the bridesmaid dresses for the wedding and these gowns for the reception?"

"Fine," I said, relief flooding through me. "That actually makes sense."

"Excellent." Aiden beamed, obviously pleased with himself, and then he finally left us to change.

"Unbelievable," I said, still trying not to think about the fortune hanging on hangers and lying across chairs. "All right, let's get these dresses on before I have a full-blown panic attack."

A few minutes later, a knock at the door pulled my focus from the sea of gowns and laughter. "What now?" I half-dreaded the answer.

"Ah, I have one last thing," Aiden said through the wood.

I swung the door open, bracing myself. He stood there, holding a tiara in his hands, a delicate circlet of metal and gemstones that glinted with an otherworldly light. Behind me, snickers and gasps rippled through the room.

"Whoa, what's that for?" I stared at the crown warily.

"Isn't it obvious? It's for you," Aiden said, as if crowning me was the most natural thing in the world.

"Look, I'm not the queen here, okay? That's Roma's job." My voice was firm, but I couldn't help being a little mesmerized by the intricate craftsmanship of the piece.

"Would you wear it if I brought one for Roma too?" He tilted his head, considering my reaction carefully.

"Fine." I resigned myself to his plan. "I suppose so."

"Perfect." His smile was triumphant, and despite everything, I shared in his joy.

Aiden's grin widened, and he reached into his messenger bag with a flourish that was all too characteristic of him. He pulled out a box of polished wood and opened it to reveal a velvet lining cradling an ancient-looking diadem. Its stones sparkled with the wisdom of ages, and the metalwork twisted like vines frozen in time.

"Thought you might say that," he said, mischief clear on his face. "I anticipated your objection."

“Roma?" I said.

She came over, her eyes round as she regarded it.

"Where did you...?" Her words trailed off as she peered closer at the relic.

"Bran's grandmother's crown. It seems an elf had a rather light pocket that became heavy during a stroll, and they only realized it when it was too late." Aiden's explanation came with a casual shrug as if such occurrences were everyday events.

Roma took a picture. I peered over her shoulder.

So, hey. Aiden says this is your grandmother's crown. Says it was 'found' by an elf. That true?

The reply came quicker than I expected.

Bran: Unfortunately, yes.

There was a pause before another message popped up.

Bran: That crown has been missing for centuries. Leave it to an elf to turn a royal heirloom into a pocket trinket.

Even through text, I could feel Bran's mixed exasperation and relief.

"Elves," I said under my breath, shaking my head. There was no denying the beauty or the sentiment. "You're giving this to Roma?"

"It's Bran and Roma's wedding gift," Aiden said, practically beaming now.

"All right then." I took the diadem carefully from the box, its weight a tangible piece of history in my hands. With a deep breath, I pivoted to hand it to Roma.

I was unable to suppress a grin as I watched Roma admiring the diadem once we were in the room and the door closed again.

12
CASSIE

I SLIPPED INTO THE CHAPEL, its stone walls holding whispers of ancient vows. The room, lit by flickering candles, cast a warm glow on the small gathering of friends.

Roma and Bran were marrying in the grand hall, but Shay and Martellus had opted for this room.

Shay stood by the door, a vision in a metallic wedding gown that seemed to flow like liquid silver around her petite frame, catching the hazy light with every subtle movement.

"Wow," I said under my breath, unable to peel my gaze from her unique dress.

"Stunning," Tanni said softly beside me.

Martellus, large and imposing with his troll lineage, waited for Shay at the makeshift altar, his violet-blue eyes softening when he looked at her. Arete, his harpy seneschal hovered near him, her wings folded gracefully, an honor guard for the king of misfits and his bride.

"Quiet now," Duncan, Shay's good friend and assistant, said softly from behind me, his voice a gentle reminder as the officiant cleared his throat.

"We are gathered here today in the presence of close friends..." the officiant said, his words simple but heavy with the weight of the moment.

Shay's fingers danced nervously along the edge of her dress, betraying the nervousness under her guarded demeanor. Martellus reached out, stilling her movements with a firm yet tender touch. Her grateful smile was brief, but it spoke loudly of their quiet bond.

"Martellus, do you take Shay to be your lawfully wedded wife?" the officiant asked.

"I do." His words echoed slightly off the stone.

"Do you, Shay, take Martellus to be your lawfully wedded husband?"

"I do," she said, her quiet voice steady, yet laced with a hint of sweetness.

"By the power vested in me, I now pronounce you husband and wife."

As they sealed their vows with a kiss, a shared sigh flowed through us. Even Bran, dignified and solemn, allowed himself a small smile. Roma leaned into him, her often hidden tender side on display for the moment.

"Let's give them some time alone," Rey said with a mischievous wink, ready to lead the charge out of the chamber.

"Agreed." Cathy looped her arm through Rey's with a laugh.

Shay and Martellus stood together as we filed past, their eyes locked in a world entirely their own.

We moved into the next room to wait as Roma changed into her wedding dress. The thirty-minute break also gave Shay time to change into her bridesmaid's dress as well as giving Shay and Martellus a minute alone before having to prepare for Roma and Bran's wedding.

The thirty minutes passed quickly, and the hush of the room gave way to the murmur of anticipation as I stepped into the grand hall. This was it, from the intimate to the grand. The ceiling soared; banners draped in regal splendor. Shay's castle transformed from a place of quiet history to one of majestic declarations.

“Geez." I took in the rows of guests that filled the space. They were a sea of finery and eager faces turned toward us, monster and human, a bridge between two worlds.

"Stick close," Cathy said beside me, her green eyes bright with excitement. Shay, now in a bridesmaid's dress like my own, gave me an encouraging nod.

"Ready?" Tanni asked, adjusting her glasses.

"Let's do this," I said.

Bran and Roma made their entrance, and it was like stepping into a painting. Roma, radiant and regal, wore a gown that seemed crafted from the dreams of queens. Ivory silk hugged her curves before cascading into a train that whispered secrets of old-world grace.

Delicate lace adorned the bodice, studded with pearls that caught the light like stars plucked from the night sky. Her full wavy hair framed her face, a dark cascade against the light fabric, and a crown of roses perched like a promise upon her head.

"Stunning," Rey whispered from his strategic position as best man, his foxlike eyes gleaming with approval.

"Absolutely." I barely recognized the solemn Bran beside her, his white hair and goblin-gray skin a statement of otherworldliness.

Christian, Harold, and Ike, Bran's goblin attendants, stood stiff and formal, an odd contrast to the lively energy of the room. Their presence was a reminder of the worlds colliding and merging within these walls.

As the officiant began, I tried to focus on the ceremony, but my gaze kept drifting. Aiden was nearby, part of the crowd yet undeniably separate. Once or twice, I caught him looking back at me, and I had to reel in my runaway thoughts.

I shook off the fantasies of a day when it might be

me standing where Roma stood, vows of everlasting love hanging in the air.

The officiant's voice softened. "Bran, do you take Roma to be your lawfully wedded wife, to rule by your side, in sickness and in health, for as long as you both shall live?"

"I do," Bran said, his voice laced with the gravity of his words.

"Roma, do you take Bran to be your lawfully wedded husband, to rule by your side, in sickness and in health, for as long as you both shall live?"

"I do," she returned, her voice firm, leaving no room for doubt.

"Rings," the officiant said, and Rey stepped forward, presenting them with a small, velvet cushion. Bran took Roma's ring, a band of silver with intricate runes, and slid it onto her finger. Roma followed suit, her hand steady as she adorned Bran with a matching band.

"By the exchange of these rings," said the officiant, "you are bound together with the strength of your love and the depth of your commitment. Let these rings be a reminder of this moment, your promises, and the ties that now join you both."

Then the officiant moved to the side. One of the goblins stepped forward, with the crown resting on a velvet pillow.

Bran faced the crowd, solemn and dignified, holding the ornate circlet aloft. It gleamed in the grand hall's light, the jewels encrusted on its surface mirroring the determination in his eyes. Roma stood still as a statue, her own gaze locked onto Bran with fierce pride.

"By the power of my reign and blood" Bran said, his voice carrying through the silent hall, "I crown you, Andromeda de Clare, Queen of the Goblins."

He lowered the crown onto Roma's head, the metal whispering against her hair. The crowd held its breath, and even the air seemed to still, acknowledging what was transpiring. Roma's shoulders squared under the crown, and she embraced her new role with a nod that was both graceful and commanding.

The couple turned to face the assembly, hands joined, their rings catching the light, a silent testament to their united front. A chorus of applause erupted, celebrating the union of two worlds, the merging of hearts and kingdoms.

"Let the festivities begin," the officiant said, and music swelled to fill the space, lifting the spirits of everyone present. For a moment longer, I watched the newly crowned queen and her king, thinking about the power of vows and the beauty found in the simplest of rituals.

The rest of the bridal party flocked together like a bevy of exotic birds, their dresses a cascade of colors that had been meticulously chosen for the grand event. I stood to one side, feeling the soft fabric of the bridesmaid dress against my skin.

"Everything looks wonderful, doesn't it?" Cathy brushed imaginary wrinkles from her gown.

"Perfect," I said, though my gaze strayed.

Across the room, the men were a contrast in their sleek black tuxes. All except Reynard, who stood out in his emerald velvet jacket – a touch of boldness in a sea of formality. He caught my eye and winked, and I couldn't help but laugh. Trust Rey to break convention.

Then there was Aiden in the front row of guests, looking every bit the part of the dashing guest. Our eyes met, and something unspoken passed between us. I quickly looked away, feeling heat creep up my neck. Not before I saw him smile. It was subtle, barely more than a twitch at the corner of his mouth, but it was there.

"Stop it, Cassie," I chastised myself silently. Today was time to be happy for Bran and Roma, celebrate their love, their ceremony. Not about fleeting gazes or what-ifs that churned in my heart.

"Hey, are you okay?" Tanni's voice pulled me back into the moment.

"Absolutely." I plastered on a smile. "Just... soaking it all in."

As I turned my attention to the festivities, my resolve wavered. I bit my lip, squashing down the quiet fantasies. Today wasn't the day for them.

13
CASSIE

Slipping out of the chapel, a sense of relief washed over me as I shed the formal attire for Aiden's gift. The gowns were breathtaking, silken fabric that hugged our forms in all the right places and yet somehow were the most comfortable thing I'd ever put on my body.

Roma's and Shay's faces lit up when they saw their dresses.

"It's so pretty. And light," Roma said.

"But I like my metal one better," Shay said softly, a small smile playing at the corners of her lips.

Together, we transformed into fairy princesses rather than a real queen and her friends. The night welcomed us onto the castle grounds, where twinkling lights and the murmur of conversation replaced the solemn vows of the day.

The DJ's equipment cast colorful shadows across the dance floor.

Aiden caught up to us, his expression relaxed. "It was smart to decade no live band. Best not to risk a competition. That could have turned this evening into a battleground rather than a celebration."

"Smart move," I said, though a part of me was curious about what an elven music duel would entail.

Probably best not to know.

The air had shifted since we were inside; the cool, threatening clouds had dispersed, revealing a canopy of stars. "Did you do something about the weather?" I asked Aiden, half-joking, as I glanced up at the clear sky.

He chuckled, the corners of his eyes crinkling with amusement. "No, that was Bran's doing." He gestured toward the goblin king. "I would have tried my hand at it, but he beat me to the punch."

"Really?" My brows rose in surprise as I looked from Bran to Aiden.

"Of course," Aiden said, his gaze softening as he met mine. "I know how important today is for your sister, and for you."

My heart fluttered against my ribs. There was something in the way Aiden looked at me, something that made me want to explore his depths. Despite everything that had happened in my first marriage, I found myself feeling wanted, feeling bold.

Aiden at the very least was up front about his differences from the human norm.

Well paid and briefed servers glided between the tables, their movements as seamless and brisk. All would get a bonus if they evaded any fighting or injury. If violence broke out, they'd been instructed to drop everything and run for shelter.

They bore platters that seemed to capture the interest of the guests: the earthy aroma of mushroom risotto mingling with the tang of soy from sushi platters.

Bran, at the wedding table, tucked into a charcuterie board with a satisfied nod. The rich shades of cured meats and the assortment of cheeses were a hit amongst the goblins and shifters.

I passed by the wedding table.

"Looks good, huh?" I nudged Roma, who sat beside Bran, glowing with the day's joy.

"Perfect," she said, attention on Bran, face alight with warmth that transcended appetite.

As laughter and conversation bloomed around us, a lone figure caught my notice. A guest, standing at the edge of the festivities, clad in a semi-translucent jumpsuit that played tricks with the light. It clung to her form like a second skin, shimmering with each subtle movement she made.

"Who's that?" I leaned toward Roma, nodding subtly toward the enigmatic guest.

She followed my gaze, her brows knitting together slightly. "Not sure. A friend of Martellus, I think?"

I considered this possibility, still worried. Riveting strangers at this event might spell trouble, which we were all trying to avoid.

I was just about to reach for a delicate piece of nigiri when I felt Aiden's presence beside me. His scent, subtle and woodsy, teased my senses before he even spoke.

"Hey, Cassie," he said, anticipation in his grin. "When do we get to dance?"

I glanced at the sushi platter, then back at him. His excitement flattered me and made me worry. "Food first. The dancing is after the meal."

He made a show of frowning. "Dancing should always come first, don't you think?"

I allowed myself a small smile, imagining his arms around me, but shook my head. "Eating is essential for most of us."

"Fine," he said dramatically, "but you owe me a dance." He winked.

For a moment, I let myself look forward to his arms around me.

As Aiden sauntered off, I turned my attention to the reception. Scanning the crowd, I noted the contrast between the revelers and the representatives from the alchemist council and brown suited MIIB agents stationed around the perimeter.

The alchemist guests had all dressed in conservative garb that contrasted with the lively atmosphere. Dark, tailored suits and high-necked dresses with not a single crease or wrinkle out of place. They stood in sharp contrast to the rest of the party's vivid colors and laughter.

There, among the shadows at the edge of the celebration, stood the MIIB agents, representing the Magical Interdimensional Investigative Bureau, silent sentinels in their nondescript brown suits. Hard to believe they were an interdimensional police force. They were practically part of the scenery, blending into the background except for the occasional glint of moonlight off their discreet earpieces.

I took a bite of risotto, enjoying the earthy flavor. Despite the joyous occasion, the presence of the MIIB was a silent reminder of the delicate balance in our world and how it stood with other worlds.

Tonight was not the time to feed anxiety about tomorrow's potential problems.

I caught Aiden watching me even across the crowd, his impatience clear. I smiled at him, swallowing down the last of my apprehension with a sip of wine. Dancing under the stars with him might be exactly what I needed.

As I dabbed the corners of my mouth with the napkin, I spotted Halo. I blinked twice, sure my eyes were deceiving me. Halo, who usually favored casual, often ripped clothing, was a vision in a white linen dress that hugged her curves. Heavy gold bangles clanked at her wrist, opposite of her usual minimalist style.

“Whoa, would you look at Halo?" I nudged Cathy, pointing discreetly.

"Who knew she could clean up so well?" Cathy nudged Rey in turn.

“Me," he said mildly. “That’s an outfit she only wears once in a long while. Look, she’s gathering the Alchemists to meet with us."

Halo led several people toward us through the thrum of conversation and clinking glasses. I recognized their leader, Evander Jones, his stature modest but presence unmistakable, strode next to her with an air of self-importance.

"Roma," Halo gestured to the lead alchemist, "this is Evander Jones."

He nodded curtly, the gold cufflinks at his wrists catching the light as he shook Roma's hand. A smile almost broke through his businesslike demeanor, but it didn't quite reach the cold blue of his eyes.

"Congratulations on your union," he said in a crisp tone.

"Thank you, Evander," Roma said, the glow of her happiness warm enough for both of them.

Leslie Andrews followed, her silver brooch shimmering against the dark purple fabric of her dress. She offered a gracious nod, her jewelry subtly hinting at hidden depths – literally, if Aiden's mention just before the wedding to me about spell-laden gemstones was true.

"Charmed," Leslie said. She seemed sincere, but it was equally obvious she was measuring us. Oddly, it was Rey's sweet smile at her that made me more nervous than Bran's neutrality or Martellus' stony indifference.

"Definitely storing spells in those trinkets," Aiden said to me as they moved on. The playful gleam on his face was gone, replaced by an interest that felt predatory as he watched them walk away.

"Are they dangerous?" I whispered back.

"Only if necessary." He took my hand.

As the alchemists made their exit, the daemon Numir, head of the Council, approached with the fluid grace of someone who knew exactly how much power he wielded. His black suit seemed to drink in the night, and his understated elegance was a contrast to the vibrant reception.

"Numir, head of the Council," Halo introduced.

"An honor," Numir said, his handshake firm, his smile practiced.

Ishtar was next, a small woman whose soft blonde curls clustered around her shoulders. Her pastel pink dress promised an innocence she likely didn't possess. Her whole appearance screamed 'I'm harmless,' but I could feel Halo bristle beside me.

"Ishtar," Halo's voice was tight, controlled.

"Delighted," Ishtar said in a sweet silky tone.

"Do you two have a history?" I asked Halo after the council members drifted away.

"Nothing to worry about now," Halo dismissed, though her eyes followed Ishtar's retreating form.

Luce, a powerful daemon known to us from a previous encounter, strode up. He cast a glare in Martellus's direction that was promptly returned. His presence was a dark note in the symphony of celebration.

"Martellus," Halo said, but the troll king merely grunted, unwilling to offer more.

"Congratulations to all," said Luce simply, then walked away before anyone could answer.

Aiden stayed close to me throughout, his body tense, ready for anything. It was both unsettling and reassuring. So much lay beneath the surface of this magical world, hidden under pleasantries and smiles.

"Lots of people seem to be on edge tonight," I said.

"Big events attract big attention." Aiden shrugged. "Focus on the celebration, Cassie."

Nodding, I turned back to where Shay and Roma were laughing together, their happiness radiant. Their joy cut through the tension, reminding me why we were all here. Seeing Shay so free from her usual haunted guardedness made me feel a success.

"Look at them," I nudged Aiden, tilting my head toward the brides. "That's what today is about."

"Exactly," Aiden said, his lips curving into a genuine smile. "Let's make sure they remember it for the joy, not the really great fight that might break out."

"Agreed." I ignored the last part of the statement. With a deep breath, I let myself lean into the moment, the laughter, and the promise of a dance under the stars.

Then I spotted Shay's parents carving through the crowd like determined starving wolves, their expressions set in that familiar, fake smile wrapped determined way that spelled trouble. I knew that look; it always preceded a conversation about money, one that Shay would do anything to avoid.

"Excuse me." I slipped past a couple swaying to the music and moving quickly to intercept them.

"Ah, Cassie!" her mother exclaimed with false cheer as I planted myself firmly in their path. "What a... lovely event."

"Isn't it just?" I beamed, mustering every ounce of fake enthusiasm I could. "The flowers alone are spectacular. Have you seen the centerpieces? Peonies, I think. Or are they dahlias?"

Her father's eyes narrowed slightly, impatient to brush past my rambling. But I forged ahead, speaking loudly enough for my voice to carry. "The cake. It's five tiers. Can you believe it? Five."

Out of the corner of my eye, I saw Shay and Martellus take the hint. They slipped away from the garden, disappearing into the safety of the castle.

"Anyway." I pretended not to notice their escape. "I heard there's going to be a fireworks display later. Or was it a fire dance? Something with fire, definitely."

Her mother's thin-lipped smile didn't reach her

eyes. "Yes, how... diverting. We were actually just looking for Shay—"

"Shay?" I feigned surprise. "Oh, I think she mentioned something about changing her shoes. Blisters, you know. Dreadful things. She might be gone for a while."

"Of course," her mother said, her tone laced with acid. "She's always been delicate."

"Must run in the family," I said with a tight smile. The less Shay had to deal with them tonight, the better.

I watched Shay's parents retreat, their shoulders rigid with silent frustration. It baffled me, why they always seemed to need money when their lifestyle suggested a surplus. Maybe it was greed or just the ugly habit of leaning on Shay, but it happened too often to be a coincidence.

"Well handled." Cathy sidled up next to me, scanning the area like she could sniff out trouble before it brewed.

"Shay's in the castle now," I said with a nod in her parents' direction. "They're up to the usual, I suspect."

"Ah," she said, her lips pressed into a thin line. "They never stop."

"Exactly." I sighed, looking around the reception. "Speaking of disorder, Rey is loose somewhere."

Cathy scanned the crowd. "With him around, there's no room for practical jokes tonight. Not unless he starts them."

"Thank god for small mercies," I said, grateful for Rey's presence. The last thing we needed was a shifter and elf prank war breaking out amidst the political tightrope we were all walking tonight.

"He'll keep it together," Cathy said, her voice low. "He promised."

"Good." I nodded, then let my gaze wander to the guests, hoping the rest of the evening would unfold without incident.

The dance floor hummed with anticipation; an open space bathed in the soft glow of strung fairy lights. Guests parted like the tide to create a pathway for the newlyweds. It was time for the first dance, and as Roma and Bran stepped onto the makeshift stage, Shay and Martellus joined them, their presence commanding yet intimate.

Bran and Roma moved together, a harmonious contrast of solemn dignity and persuasive charm. Nearby, Shay and Martellus found their rhythm, her golden hair reflecting the light, his horns almost regal in this setting. They were all so different, goblin and human, sybil and troll, yet together they painted a picture of unity that transcended realms.

"Can you believe how well they fit together?" whispered Cathy beside me.

"Every wedding should feel like this," I said, unable to tear my eyes away from the couples. "Like magic made visible."

"Roma's radiant." Cathy glanced at me. "And Bran... he's got the whole noble warrior king vibe down pat."

"Shay's practically glowing." Shay leaned into Martellus, her sweet, rarely seen smile a quiet secret shared between them. "For a big guy Martellus is surprisingly light on his feet."

"Who would've thought trolls could dance like that?" Cathy chuckled.

"Anyone who's fought them. Trolls are fast on their

feet." Aiden stood next to us, unnoticed until that moment.

"Not going to think about that." A warmth spread through me, a reflection of their joy. "All this almost makes you believe in fairy tales, doesn't it?"

"Definitely," she said. "This wedding is right out of one."

The DJ transitioned to a slower melody, and Aiden held out his hand with a roguish grin. "Shall we?"

"Yes," I decided, placing my hand in his. The air was thick with the scent of all the floral arrangements as he led me onto the makeshift dance floor. His hands found my waist, and mine rested on his shoulders. We began to move to the music, our bodies swaying in time with the soothing beat.

Around us, couples floated by in their own little worlds. There was something intimate about sharing the space with others yet feeling entirely alone with him. The gentle press of Aiden's palms through the fabric of my gown anchored me, and the tension in my shoulders melted away.

"Everyone seems to have forgotten the world outside this dance floor," I said.

"Good," Aiden said, his blue eyes holding mine. "Tonight should be for celebration, not combat."

Laughter bubbled up from the crowd, and I smiled in response. It was infectious, this joy. For a moment, it didn't matter what came next or what had passed. There was only here and now, and the warmth of Aiden's touch.

My attention drifted momentarily to the edge of the dance area, where I caught sight of Halo, her expression sour, being lured into the dance by Edward. His hand was gently placed on her lower back, guiding rather than forcing. I raised an eyebrow, wondering at the mix of determination and gentleness in his approach.

"How did he manage that?" I said softly to Aiden, nodding slightly toward them.

"Daemons can be persuasive," Aiden said with a chuckle. "Given her stubbornness and dislike for them are legendary, I'm curious too."

"Or maybe she just couldn't resist his charm." I glanced back at the unlikely pair. Edward whispered something in her ear, and to my surprise, a feral smile tugged at Halo's lips.

"Perhaps." Aiden spun me gently. "But I wouldn't bet on it."

The music shifted, a melody weaving through the night air that spoke of enchantment and dreams. Aiden's hand tightened on mine, his other arm wrapping securely around my waist. We swayed in unison, our steps slow and measured to the rhythm.

"Are you okay?" he asked, his breath brushing my cheek and ear. The sensation made me shiver.

"More than okay." I moved my head so my cheek rested lightly against his shoulder. I breathed in the subtle scent of him, earthy and grounding. The rest of the world, with its complexities and shadows, old anxieties and angers, seemed to dissolve into the background.

"Good." His breath was warm on my skin. "Because right now, this moment is all that matters."

I couldn't disagree. There was a purity in the simplicity of movement, the tenderness of the music, the softness of his grip. It was as if we were the only two people in existence, dancing on a cloud or in some secret place where time stood still.

Probably best not to mention it. I probably didn't want to find out what dancing in a cloud felt like in real life.

His fingers brushed along my back, sending a shiver through me that had nothing to do with the cool night air. My heart fluttered, but not from fear or anxiety, it was anticipation, a yearning for the unknown that lay ahead with him.

"Stay with me, Cassie," he whispered, almost as if he had read my thoughts.

"I hope to," I said. It was the best I could offer, and from his smile, he was more than willing to accept it.

The song twined around us, binding us together in its gentle embrace. Just like that, I was lost, lost in the music, lost in the warmth of Aiden's presence, lost in a dance that felt like a promise of hope.

14
CASSIE

After the dance Aiden slipped away and I moved near one of the decorative pillars. The clinking of glasses and the murmur of conversation filled the air as I watched the reception unfold.

The alchemist Evander Jones was in his element, surrounded by a few admirers eager to catch a snippet of his wisdom.

Unease that prickled the back of my neck – something was about to shift.

"Evander," came a call, sharp enough to slice through the chatter. It belonged to one of the Council aides, a man with a face as forgettable as his name. "A word. About the Formless Ones."

Evander turned and he nodded once. The small crowd parted for him; he beckoned Leslie Andrews with a flick of his wrist before striding toward a grouping of tables. Leslie tossed me a smug look as if this secret meeting would elevate her beyond our petty concerns.

"Numir will see you now." The aide allowed Evander and Leslie to pass before moving to my side. "They've requested you join them."

"Me?" I asked, my surprise genuine. The aide didn't wait for a response, just gestured for me to follow.

The tension in the air was a tangible thing, pressing against my skin as I saw the others moving toward the meeting area.

The Kings.

Bran's solemn attention was fixed ahead, his long white hair like a silent banner of his dignity. Rey, with that mischievous expression, seemed almost to dance around the seriousness of our procession. Martellus walked with the steady grace of someone who is used to being underestimated because of his size. Hugh, who cultivated not being noticed successfully enough, this was the first time I'd spotted him at the reception.

We reached the tables of seated daemons. That's when Hugh stopped dead, his broad back going rigid. The muscles in his jaw clenched visibly.

"Something wrong?" Martellus rumbled, his voice low enough that it wouldn't carry to the tables.

Hugh didn't turn to face us. "I can't... It's not right."

"Can't what?" Rey prodded.

"Meet with them." There was a tremor in Hugh's reply, a hint of the struggle happening beneath his controlled exterior. His eyes had shaded to red, a gleam in the darkness

Evander approached from behind, passing by me with that signature confident stride. He leaned close to Hugh, his smile cold. "You're letting your fears dictate your actions, Hugh. Your woman is safe from us for the moment."

For a moment, Hugh's eyes flared bright red, a silent warning of the beast within wrestling for control. My heart skipped. This wasn't just a disagreement; this could turn into something dangerous.

"Go," Bran's voice was soft but carried an edge that sliced through the tension. "I'll handle this. And I will tolerate no threat to Tanni."

Without another word, Hugh turned and strode away, leaving us to stare after him. The fear that clutched at my throat made it difficult to swallow. We were on the brink, and it felt like any move could send us tumbling into hullabaloo.

"Evander. Do not threaten her again, even by implication." Bran's controlled voice stopped the tension left in Hugh's wake. His white hair caught the dim light, giving him an otherworldly aura.

Evander simply shrugged, the epitome of nonchalance. "A vampire like Hugh must maintain a tight grip on his control. It's for his own good, and ours."

His words, smooth and assured, wrapped around the room like velvet. I shivered despite myself. It was unsettling, how Evander's confidence made something so cruel sound almost reasonable, likable even. A chill crept down my spine, reminiscent of the iron grasp Franklin's potions once had on me.

"Are you okay?" Aiden asked, noticing my discomfort.

I nodded, but reached for his hand anyway, seeking warmth. "Just got a bit cold all of a sudden."

I gripped Aiden's hand tighter as we seated ourselves with the alchemists and council members. Silence fell around us, the sounds of the reception fading.

"Let us dispense with pleasantries," Numir said, his face cold and hard. "The current situation is dire. We propose a sacrifice of those humans gifted with potent magic to the Formless Ones to make an agreement for them to leave this world."

"Gifted humans?" I whispered, feeling Aiden's hand tense around mine.

"Indeed." Evander leaned forward, his dark eyes glinting. "You want to serve humanity up on a silver platter to those... things?"

"Better them than us," Ishtar said quietly. It took a moment for her words to sink in, delivered in her sweet calm tones

"Your plan is barbaric," I couldn't keep the disgust from my expression.

"Barbarism is a matter of perspective," Numir said smoothly. "Especially when survival is at stake."

"Survival? You mean your own," said Aiden.

Evander snorted. "Easy for you to say, since you're not under any threat. Elf."

"Enough," Bran said, his authoritative tone demanding silence. "Evander, explain exactly what your endgame is. What alternative do you offer to save humanity."

"Simple," Evander said. "We've been working to expel you monsters, to reduce the overall magical footprint of this world. Then you came back, like a case of warts."

"To make it unappealing for the Formless Ones," I said, understanding dawning on me.

"Exactly," Leslie Andrews said, her condescension palpable. "It's about controlling the variables."

"Control," Rey said. "At what cost? Your means have nearly destroyed the trolls and vampires, and brutalized Bran's and my people."

"Whatever it takes," Evander said firmly, clasping his hands. "We face reality. For humanity to survive, there's no room for you here."

"Both your plans reek of cowardice," Martellus's words fell like stones.

"Does it?" Numir said, the facade of civility crumbling. "Or does it speak of necessity? You, like the elf, can flee to another world. We can't."

"Enough." I couldn't contain my revulsion. "Destroying whole races is awful. Feeding people to your enemies as sacrifices is monstrous. You're both terrible."

"Monstrous," Leslie sneered. "That's rich, coming from someone who's playing the toy to an elf."

"Better to be a monster than a murderer," Bran said.

"You are all fools," Ishtar said, her sweet voice slicing through the tension. She stood abruptly, her chair scraping violently against the floor. "We're done here."

"Wait—" Evander's attempt at persuasion fell on deaf ears as the council members stormed out, their departure leaving a charged silence in their wake.

"Formless Ones don't play favorites, they'll take anyone they can," Aiden broke the quiet, his tone serious. "Franklin's possession is proof enough. They're already here. He's cooperating with them, you've said. That makes the situation more precarious."

"Which means we need to act." The weight of the situation settled around us.

"Right," he nodded. "If the alchemists and monsters worked together, maybe we'd stand a chance."

"An alliance?" Evander crossed his arms. "It's not what we planned, but perhaps it's time for a new strategy."

"Perhaps indeed," Bran said with a heavy sigh.

A moment stretched, heavy and expectant. Evander cleared his throat, the sound somehow settling the angry atmosphere left by the council's dramatic exit.

"Then it's settled," he said, voice oddly resonant in the quiet that enveloped us. "We will join forces with you monsters, against the Formless Ones."

He turned to Martellus, an unspoken challenge hanging in the air. "We mean it this time."

I shifted uncomfortably. Aiden stood next to me, a statue dedicated to suspicion. Bran's expression remained stoic and unreadable, but I caught the briefest flicker of doubt cross Roma's face before she masked it with her usually assured facade.

"Evander," Martellus said, the room hanging on his gravelly tone, "your words have proven... hollow in the past."

Evander nodded, a concession. "True. Necessity breeds sincerity. Our survival is bound to yours now."

"Survival has a way of changing perspectives," Leslie said, her arrogance softened somewhat by the gravity of our plight.

"Doesn't mean we trust you," Roma cut in sharply, arms crossed.

"Nor should you," Rey said from the doorway.

"Trust is earned," Bran finally spoke, grounding us. "Not given freely, especially not now."

"Agreed," I said, feeling the cold edge of skepticism within me. "What choice do we have?"

"None," Aiden said, his hand squeezing mine. "It's this or let the Formless Ones eat your world."

"Then let's begin." Leslie stepped forward, extending a well-manicured hand toward Martellus.

He stared at it for a beat too long before grasping it. "For now, we fight together."

15
CASSIE

I WAS BACK MINGLING among the guests, a flute of champagne forgotten in my hand when I noticed the mirrors. They were small, ornate things, scattered throughout the reception area, catching flickers of laughter and light. At first glance, they seemed like nothing more than cleverly placed decor to add to the enchantment of Roma and Shay's special day.

"Are you enjoying the evening?" an elf asked, pride in his movement as he gestured toward one of the mirrors.

"Are those magic?" I asked, a frown creasing my forehead.

"Indeed," he said with a flourish. "Our little contribution." He tapped the mirror and it sprung to life, revealing not just our reflections but images that fluttered past too quickly to grasp. Confused, I leaned closer.

"Wait, what are those?" I said, as fragmented scenes danced across the surface – a young boy stealing an apple, a couple locked in an embrace, a woman weeping silently in a dark room.

"Memories, truths, emotions," he said. "The mirrors capture the essence of everyone they reflect."

I felt a cold pit form in my stomach as I watched the elf pluck a smaller mirror from the air, its surface alive with the recorded secrets of unsuspecting guests. Laughter bubbled around us as the miniature mirrors began circulating, each revelation a source of amusement for the elegant crowd.

"Stop this," I hissed, anger rising within me. "This is invasive. This is awful."

"How?" The elf looked genuinely puzzled. "Look at this love." He pointed to a mirror showcasing two guests.

"Enough." I snatched a mirror from a passing tray. My own reflection stared back at me before shifting to reveal moments of vulnerability I'd buried deep – and there it was, a still image of me gazing at Aiden with raw desire painted across my face.

"Give me that." I tried to snatch the mirror away, but it slipped through my fingers and shattered on the floor, the fragments winking out one by a time.

"Where is Aiden's?" I trembled with fear and rage.

"Lost in the festivities, perhaps," the elf said, indifferent to my distress.

I turned away, struggling to compose myself. If these creatures, related to the Formless Ones, could pull off something like this, what could our declared enemies do? My heart raced with unease. Elves had stripped us bare without a second thought. What else were their cousins capable of?

"Enjoy the rest of the evening," the elf called after me, oblivious to the turmoil churning inside me. Enjoyment was the farthest thing from my mind now.

I strode to where Aiden waited, at the edge of the crowd.

"Tell me you didn't know about this," I said through gritted teeth, my hands balled into fists at my sides.

Aiden's jaw clenched, a clear sign of frustration. "Of course, I didn't," he said, the blue intensity of his eyes burning. "Cassie, I'm not perfect. They came up with what they thought would be a pleasant surprise."

"Then why are they here? Why risk it?" I spoke hard and quietly, not wanting to disrupt the reception.

"Because we are willing to defend this world too," Aiden said, his tone sharp. "I wish... just once, you'd stop judging us by the actions of other people."

"Elves exposed everyone's secrets for fun," I said, unable to contain the storm of my fears.

"Later, Cassie," he said.

Turning on his heel, Aiden strode briskly away from the reception. He whistled, and Cu came running. A moment later Aiden was mounted.

"Where are you going?" I called after him, my anger turning to desperation.

"Taking some air. I'll be back if you need aid with the cleanup. If you'll allow an elf to help you." Cu launched himself into the air.

"Of course. Leave the discussion," I said to no one, watching his figure vanish into the sky. Alone now, hurt settled heavily on my shoulders.

As the last of the guests trickled out into the evening, I found myself staring at a small mirror left abandoned on a table. It no longer showed images of the past, but my own reflection, tired eyes and frown lines etched deep into my face. My panicked temper had faded, leaving behind a hollow feeling of regret.

"Hey," Roma's presence interrupted my self-reflection. She's changed into normal clothing and was wiping down another table, her movements efficient. "You did good today, Cass. Despite... everything."

"Did I?" I half-scoffed, placing the mirror face down. "I lost it at Aiden. For what? Some elf misstep, one of hundreds.?"

She stopped her work and sat beside me. She gave me a quick hug. "It was more than a misstep for you, wasn't it?"

I shrugged, unable to meet her gaze. "Maybe. I shouldn't have gotten so worked up."

Roma placed her hand on mine. "Can I say something, and you promise not to bite my head off?"

"Depends on what it is," I said, though my attempt at levity fell flat. "It's your wedding day, so I'll try hard not to."

"You've went through hell with Franklin," she said, her tone gentle yet firm. "Manipulated, controlled... it'd leave anyone with scars. Maybe seeing those mirrors, feeling exposed, it stirred up your need to push back, to assert control?"

I let out a slow breath, her words settling in. "You think I'm still reacting to him, even now?"

"Maybe not directly to him." She squeezed my hand. "To what he represents. The fear of being vulnerable, of someone else pulling the strings. Of being in prison with your mind so messed with you don't even know you're in prison."

I leaned back, the breeze carrying whispers of conversations from departing guests. Roma was right. I had built walls so high I couldn't even see when someone was genuinely trying to help, or just be close. Like Aiden.

"Thanks," I said, a genuine smile touching the corners of my mouth. "For putting up with me."

"Always." She stood up and resuming her work. "Now, let's finish this cleanup so we can get some rest. We both need it."

"Right behind you." I found new resolve to make amends. With Roma by my side, I felt a little less alone against the chaos of my own making.

The twilight deepened, casting a violet hue over the reception grounds. I weaved through tables, helping the servers collecting discarded plates, my thoughts a tangled mess.

Aiden wasn't Franklin; he didn't have that worm's knack for manipulation. As I passed a few elves lingering nearby, their laughter tinkling like wind chimes, I felt it, their magic. It oozed charisma, making it hard to stay mad or even remember why I should be.

"Hey, Cassie," said Matilda, and I turned to see her approaching. "You're doing great, you know."

"Thanks." I tried not to get sucked in by the warmth in her words. It was just their magic at work, not real camaraderie.

"Come on, smile. It's a party after all." He grinned, and for a second, I almost forgot myself and smiled back. Then I remembered Aiden, how I'd lashed out at him, and my face hardened.

"Stop it," I said curtly, moving away.

I was stacking glasses onto a tray when the alarm blared, a sound so alien and jarring against the evening's merriment. My heart leaped into my throat. Everyone remaining froze for a moment.

"What the—" I said, but the rest of my question was drowned out by the rising clamor.

"Attack!" The shout came from the shoreline, where Rey and Cathy were standing. Two of the MIIB agents were there as well.

"Attack?" Panic flared up in me as a few human guests scrambled to their feet, confusion painting their faces.

Monster guests were producing weapons left and right, which didn't help with the human guests' panic.

"Everyone, please remain calm." I tried to project authority I didn't feel, clambering onto a nearby chair. "We'll handle this."

Inside, I was reeling. Attack? Now? With everyone still here?

"Find shelter," someone else cried, and the crowd surged toward the portal like a startled flock of birds. Which wasn't bad, it was probably safer there right now.

"Roma!" I shouted, searching for her in the chaos. We needed to organize, protect the guests, figure out—

"Here." she yelled back, already directing some guests toward the portal.

"Listen to Roma." I commanded anyone who would listen, and then I was off, running toward the alarm, toward whatever threat loomed over us.

This was no time for personal turmoil. This was a time for action. Yet, even as I sprinted forward, my mind flickered unwillingly to Aiden—wherever he was—and I cursed myself for still caring.

I darted between the tables overturned in the panic, my ears ringing with the alarm's echo. Above me, the sky darkened, a tangible omen of the Council's disapproval. "They're mad we've allied with the alchemists," Bran hissed as he joined me, his strides urgent and long. 'You should get to safety inside the building. You're prime hostage material."

"Alchemists?" My tone was sharp with disbelief. "Why—"

"Because of us." The words came from Arete, her wings casting grand shadows on the ground as she landed gracefully among the disorder, her amber eyes fierce. "The Council fears our presence here."

"Monsters are not Formless Ones." I spat out the words. "Why can't they see that there are other options?"

"Perception is reality to them," Martellus rumbled, appearing beside Arete with Shay in tow. "Our alliance has tipped their scales."

"Roma," I called again, needing her clarity in this tumult of fear and frustration. She ran toward us, having ushered the last of the guests through the portal to safety.

"Monsters, alchemists, elves," Roma counted off on her fingers, her expression calm and steady. "A cocktail for threat to the Council. We need to show them we're powerful enough not to mess with."

"Convince a Council that's set on seeing us as destroyers?" Arete scoffed, her talons digging into the earth. "Futile."

"Then we prepare for battle," Martellus said, his tone like a sword being drawn. "It's their move now."

16
CASSIE

The air shimmered, and then all hell broke loose. Bright edged portals snapped open like gaping maws across the grounds where we had gathered, each one spewing out followers of the Council in droves. They came prepared, armed with an arsenal of spells and bizarre, snarling creatures.

"Get down!" I yelled, as a swarm of fireballs shot overhead, leaving trails of acrid smoke behind them. Others dove for cover as I ducked, the heat singing the tips of my hair.

I glanced at Bran, who stood tall amidst the havoc, his white hair shining against the darkening sky, a blade in hand.

Where on earth had he gotten it?

His eyes, usually so calm and reflective, burned with fierce resolve. "Roma."

She was already back on her feet, her black hair whipping around her face like a war banner. Her face was ablaze with a determination that matched his. Together, they were a formidable front against the onslaught.

It wasn't just fireballs and strange creatures we had to worry about. The Council knew the weaknesses of the various monster peoples, and they exploited them without mercy. Glistening vials arched through the air, breaking open upon impact. A green mist enveloped several of the goblins in our ranks, and my heart sank as their forms blurred and shrank, leaving behind a cluster of confused bunnies twitching their noses amid the tumult.

Goblins were vulnerable to shapeshifting magic, something they tried to keep very quiet.

"Damn it," Roma cursed, rushing toward the newly transformed goblins. "Hold on, you'll be okay."

The sight was ludicrous, fluffy bunnies hopping between spells and stomping feet, but the implications were terrifying. If The Council could do this to the goblins, what else were they capable of? More importantly, how many more surprises did they have up their sleeves?

I scrambled to my feet, my thoughts racing. We needed to turn the tide, and quickly. As I looked around at the faces of those I loved, those who had come together for what should have been a celebration, I realized we were fighting not just for survival, but for the right for humanity not to be sold to the invading energy beings.

"Back-to-back. Don't let them surround us!" I shouted, hoping my voice could pierce through the noise. We needed to regroup, reassess. First, we had to win.

I gasped, my eyes wide as Bran, the dignified king of goblins, parried a sapphire potion flung at him with his sword. With a flourish that defied explanation, he produced another massive weapon in his other hand, its blade glinting with a deadly light.

The council followers recoiled as Bran approached. He had no place to hide such a monstrosity; it was as if the sword had materialized from the very air itself.

"Roma, focus on the bunnies," I yelled, trying to keep track of her as she darted among the confused creatures. Her voice, usually sharp and commanding, took on a soothing cadence that seemed to weave through the disorder. "You're stronger than this illusion," she coaxed. "Remember who you are."

One by one, the bunnies shivered, their forms wavering before snapping back into the proud figures of goblin warriors. Roma's persuasive magic, laced with a hidden tenderness, worked to undo the Council's cruel mind magic.

"Keep it up, Roma!" I shouted encouragement, but my attention was pulled away by a new threat.

"Look out, Hugh!" Tanni screamed.

A glass vial shattered at the feet of my friend Hugh, the vampire king. A dark red mist billowed up, and Hugh's normally restrained demeanor fractured. His eyes turned a deep crimson, and he snarled menacingly.

"Stop him!" I cried out, but it was too late. Hugh lunged at the nearest council member, his movements a blur of primal hunger. The man's scream was cut short as Hugh's bloodlust took over.

Tanni was at his side in an instant, assessing the situation even as her body acted on instinct. "Hugh! You have to fight it." She grappled with him. "Cassie, help me. He'll be devastated when he comes to his senses."

I rushed to their side, knowing full well the remorse that would crush Hugh once the potion's effect waned. Guilt was a heavy burden. Hugh didn't deserve this. As I helped Tanni try to restrain him, I thought of all the times we'd fought together, side by side against the darkness. Now, here we were, fighting against the darkness within.

There was no way we could physically stop the steel hard muscle under our hands. Tanni was stronger than a normal human, and Hugh didn't budge, drinking deep from the vein.

"Stay with us, Hugh." I hoped my voice could reach him. "We need you."

Amid the chaos, I found Rey, a blur of orange and white fur as he morphed into a tiger mid-leap, pouncing with the ferocity that only the king of shapeshifters could muster. His prowess was short-lived; a council member, with the precision of a practiced thrower, launched a canister at Rey's feet. It erupted into a cloud of treated wolfsbane, the fine particles glittering menacingly in the sunlight.

"Rey!" I shouted.

His roar turned to a painful cough, and his majestic leap faltered as he stumbled to the ground, shaking his great feline head in distress.

Cathy, ever the quick thinker, darted forward. "Hold on, Rey!" she cried out, her green eyes flashing with concern. Without hesitation, she unscrewed a water bottle and drenched his snout, washing away traces of wolfsbane as if she was extinguishing a fire.

"Come on, big guy," Cathy said, her voice both soothing and commanding.

With the crisis surrounding Rey momentarily in hand, I turned my attention to the battlefield, just in time to see Martellus towering over the fray. He wielded a colossal battle hammer that seemed to appear from thin air. The weapon looked ancient, its handle wrapped in worn leather and its head etched with runes. Where did it come from? There was no place for such a monstrous thing to hide on him.

Shay stood next to him, eyes wide with distress. Her lips moved and Martellus ducked his head listening.

I was going to find out where the heck these men had been hiding those weapons.

Before he could respond, a council member lobbed another potion, its contents sparkling with malicious intent. The vial shattered against Martellus's chest, and in a flash of light, both he and Shay vanished, leaving nothing but a faint echo of their surprised shouts.

"Martellus! Shay!" My words were useless, they were gone. Disbelief rooted me to the spot for a precious second, my thoughts racing. What kind of spell could've—

I ducked as a swooping mass of shadow and fang lunged at where my head had been. The lesser daemons, once cloaked in the guise of men, now unfurled into their true, monstrous forms, a nightmare cadre of the Council's entourage.

"Edward. What are you doing? Fight!" One of the council members, wrapped in a cloak that shimmered like oil on water, barked at the daemon who stood apart from the fray.

"I won't be part of this," Edward said, his arms folded. His mouth was set in a grim line, his red hair like fire against the anarchy. "This is wrong."

"You're a fool. This is our chance." The council member gestured at us with disgust.

"Maybe I feel this is a stupid choice," he said, arms crossed, defiance etched in every line of his body.

The battle raged around us, a cacophony of clashing spells and cries. I was about to dive back in when something inside me snapped. Too much. It was just too much.

"Stop!" The word was more than a command, it was a surge, a wave of power that rippled through the air. A level of magic I never knew I had.

It worked. Everyone froze. Weapons paused mid-strike. Potions hung in the air, their deadly contents suspended. Even the lesser daemons' snarls died in their throats.

"Stand down!" My words echoed, as if spoken by a chorus, not just me.

With a sudden pop, Martellus and Shay reappeared. He was as imposing as ever, dressed in mail with his hammer clenched in his right hand; she was, impossibly, shockingly, cradling a swollen belly under a long loose floor length green dress.

"Shay..." My jaw dropped. How?

The silence stretched, everyone's attention fixed on the couple. For a moment, the air was full of confusion.

"Shay?" I stepped forward. "What happened?"

Martellus, hammer forgotten at his side, placed a protective arm around her. Shay looked up, her brown eyes wide but clear, her face serene despite the bedlam that had raged just seconds ago.

"Later," she said softly. "We'll explain later."

For now, that was enough. She was safe. They both were. For the first time, I allowed myself to believe that maybe, just maybe, I had real power after all.

Aiden burst through the throng of halted combatants, dragging a disheveled and protesting Franklin by the collar. His eyes found mine across the battlefield-turned-tableau.

"I've got him." He interrupted the surrounding silence.

I blinked, taking in Franklin's flabby form and the triumphant glint in Aiden's eyes. "You went after him?" I asked, not quite processing the scene before me.

"Figured it was time someone proved they're not like him. Also, you can communicate with the Formless Ones through him, since he's possessed by them," Aiden said with a nod toward Franklin, who squirmed under his grasp.

My attention snapped back to Shay, still rubbing her belly in the classic pregnant woman gesture. Confusion swirled inside me, a tornado threatening to uproot what little calm I had mustered.

"What happened?" I asked, my words less an inquiry and more a squawk of confusion.

Shay's amused eyes met mine. "We were banished to Dream with that spell," she said. "Couldn't get back..." She shrugged. "Time runs differently there. Especially if Dream doesn't want you to leave."

I shook my head, unable to reconcile the timeline. "It's only been a few minutes here."

"Eight and a half months there." She patted her stomach with a tender smile. "As for what happened, when a mommy and a daddy love each other very much..."

I rolled my eyes, but Roma snickered.

The reality of her words hit me harder than any physical blow could have. If Dream had done this to Martellus, who dealt with them on a routine basis, what would they have done with me if I'd visited?

I looked at Martellus, then back at Shay, and something fierce and protective welled up inside me. I wanted those I cared for to be safe. We needed to do something about the invasion.

"All right." I left no room for argument. "Let's sort this mess out."

The air hummed with the tension of a battlefield gone silent, the ground littered with remnants of spells cast and potions shattered. I stood firmly, my focus locked onto Franklin, who was now subdued but still wore that little smug smirk that made my blood boil.

Aiden's grip on Franklin's collar was ironclad, and there was a question in his eyes as he looked over to me for direction.

Before I could speak, one of the MIIB agents, their presence unexpected amidst such disorder, stepped forward with authority that seemed to come from years of dealing with the arcane and the dangerous.

"Execution is not necessary," he said, his voice firm and decisive. "He will face justice for his crimes through due process."

Their agents moved through the scene with practiced ease, securing council members and attackers alike with restraints woven of magic stronger than any steel. Spells were neutralized, creatures contained, and order began to claw its way back from the brink of madness.

"Is that what you want, Cassie?" Aiden asked. My heart raced at the decision. Yes, Franklin had hurt me, scarred me in ways that might never fully heal, but this... this was bigger than us.

"Yes," I said without hesitation. "Let the law handle him. I'll be happy to help question him later."

Aiden gave a curt nod and released Franklin into the custody of the MIIB agents, who handled him with a cold impersonal professionalism. As they led him away, Aiden turned back to me, something shifting in his posture, a momentary vulnerability.

He reached into his shirt pocket and pulled out a small, ornate mirror. "For you." He pressed it into my hands.

Confusion filled me as I took the mirror, its surface gleaming with the dim light.

"Watch it," he said gently.

My fingers trembling, I tapped the mirror with a touch, and the memories within unfolded before my eyes. There he was, Aiden, looking into the mirror with an intensity that made my breath catch. His thoughts and desires didn't need sound to convey their meaning. His stance, his expression, everything about him screamed the truth I hadn't dared to believe.

He loved me.

I clutched the mirror close, the realization washing over me like a wave, warm and relentless. It was a moment of clarity that soothed old scars, a point of certainty in a world full of mayhem. For the first time since I discovered what Franklin had done to me, I allowed myself to feel the full weight of my emotions, and hope for the possibility of a future worth fighting for.

Aiden held out his hand, palm up, and with a gesture that felt too elegant for the battlefield we stood on, summoned something from the ether. A tiny, luminescent vial materialized, hovering just above his skin. It was sealed with intricate filigree, glowing subtly with an inner light.

"An elixir of longevity," he said, his voice a low thrum that seemed to resonate in the space between us. "For you."

"But... elves don't share these. Ever." The knowledge sat heavy on my tongue, a fact learned from the price paid for the one awaiting Roma's decision to drink.

"True," he acknowledged, his piercing blue gaze holding mine. "But I want you to have it. No strings attached, no expectations. A true gift."

The gravity of his words settled, a weight of power and sacrifice. Elves guarded their secrets as fiercely as they did their lives, the cost to him must be immense.

"Thank you." I reached out to take the vial, feeling its cool surface against my fingertips. I tucked it safely into my pocket, the glass nestling against the fabric like a promise.

"Will you stay?" I asked abruptly, the question driven by a newfound courage. "After all this, after we defeat the Formless Ones, will you stay for other tasks? There might be more I'll need help with."

Aiden's smile was slow and sweet, spreading across his features like the dawn breaking over a darkened horizon.

"Yes," he said, simple and sure.

17
RISSA

I PERCHED on the edge of the park bench, near the ocean, a breeze tugging at my hair as dusk settled over the city. The stink of the Council's magic still hung in the air, its reek a reminder of the line I had drawn in the sand. My mind churned with memories, each one a bitter pill.

"Never again," I said to myself.

"Talking to yourself, Rissa?" A familiar voice cut through the twilight, tinged with amusement.

Edward stepped out of the shadows, his red hair like a flare in the dim light. I suppressed a shiver; not from the cold, but from the complicated mix of emotions his presence always stirred within me.

This once, violence might not be the correct answer, even though it had served me well in the past.

"Only because I find my own company more palatable than most people's." I kept my tone even.

He took a seat beside me, his ice-blue eyes meeting mine. Caution lived in his gaze, a delicate dance between what he was and who he wanted to be. "They're rotten to the core. You know it, I know it."

"Of course, they are." A trace of venom seeped into my words as I remembered their plan. "Breeding humans for magic, only to leave them helpless against... against things that should never have come here."

"Formless ones," he offered the term quietly, almost reverently.

"Monsters," I corrected sharply.

"Monsters," he said, a flicker of agreement in his tone. "That's why I've been looking for you. We need to put an end to this."

"By 'we.'" I narrowed my eyes at him. "Do you mean me? Because your lot doesn't exactly inspire trust."

The corners of his well-trimmed beard lifted in a half-smile. "I can't blame you for that. But yes, you. You turned down a spot on the Council, ages ago. You see through their lies."

"Still, that doesn't mean I'm signing up for your revolution." I stood abruptly. The last rays of sunlight dipped below the horizon, casting us both in half-shadow.

"Listen or don't, Rissa. This isn't going away." His face was solemn now, earnest in a way that made it harder to dismiss him outright. "Neither am I."

"Damn it." I cursed under my breath. "I'll hear what you have to say. That's all I'm promising."

"Fair enough." He stood too, the tension between us a tangible thing. "For what it's worth, I hope you do join us. The Council needs to fall, and you... you could be the tipping point."

"Or a sacrifice." I thought to their despicable plans. As I walked away, leaving him standing in the growing darkness, I couldn't shake the feeling that maybe, just maybe, I was already part of his revolution.

The crunch of gravel under my boots was a welcome sound after the tension-soaked conversation with Edward. My little house, tucked among the forested hills just beyond the reach of Los Angeles' glow, stood silent and unassuming. I fumbled for my keys, still mulling over Edward's words, his earnestness, the weight of his words. Damn him for not being easy to dismiss.

Inside, I tossed my jacket on the hook and made a beeline for the kitchen counter where I had left the folder from the dating agency. The idea seemed ludicrous now, finding some semblance of normalcy and family in a world teetering on the edge of upheaval. There it was, the paper folder, an absurd promise of mundane romance.

I flipped it open, and son of a bitch. There he was. Edward's name at the top of my matches. A bitter laugh escaped me, and I swore under my breath, the sound sharp in the quiet room. It was like fate itself was mocking me, pushing me toward the very person I had kept at arm's length for a very long time.

"Of course." I stared at the perfectly typed letters

that spelled out his name. "Because why make it simple?"

The phone rang, slicing through my irritation with its shrill insistence. I snatched it up, "Hello?"

"Rissa Halo?" The voice on the other end was crisp, businesslike.

"Speaking."

"This is Agent Marks with the MIIB. We have a situation concerning the Council. Your... expertise is required."

"Is that so?" I leaned against the counter, thumbing the edge of the folder. "What makes you think I'm interested in playing liaison?"

"Your past interactions with them make you an ideal candidate. We are aware of your... unique perspective."

"Great." No good deed, indeed. I let out a slow breath, pinching the bridge of my nose. "When do we start?"

"Tomorrow morning, Ms. Halo. We'll send a car."

"Can't wait." The sarcasm dripped heavy even to my own ears. I hung up without a goodbye and stared at Edward's name again.

"Looks like you're going to get your wish," I said to the empty room. "You wanted me involved, Edward? You got it." Whether that would be a victory for him or the final nail in an already closing coffin, only time would tell.

MORE FICTION BY DAPHNE MORE

https://daphnekmoore.com/books

Midlife Magic Dating Service

Monsters Matchmaking

Trying the Trickster

Vetting the Vampire

Testing the Troll

Midlife Mage

Complete Series

Unfazed

Unbowed

Unsaid

Uncaged

Set in the Midlife Mage Universe:

The Reckoning

Unwanted

Unrepentant

Unbroken

ABOUT DAPHNE MOORE

Daphne Moore has been a storyteller from her preliterate days. She writes them down now for those out of earshot. She writes what she loves—speculative fiction in all forms, with a seasoning of romance.

Read More from Daphne Moore

Visit her website for a free story.

www.daphnekmoore.com

MORE PARANORMAL WOMEN'S FICTION BY L.A. BORUFF

Other Series by L.A. Boruff

An Unseen Midlife

Witching After Forty

Fanged After Forty

Hunting After Forty

Godmother Training Academy

Wears Valley Witches

Midlife Magic Dating Service

Midlife Mage

Sisterhood of the Stones

Immortal West

The Meowing Medium

An Immortal Midlife

Cornellis Island Paranormal Cozy Mysteries

Bellarose Cat Cafe

Shifting Into Midlife

Primetime of Life

Magical Midlife in Mystic Hollow

The Firehouse Feline

L.A. Boruff writing as Lainie Anderson

Demons & Demigods

Southern Soil

Collective World

Coven's End

Academy's Rise

Lucifer's War

Valentine Pride

Magic & Metaphysics Academy

ABOUT L.A. BORUFF

L.A. (Lainie) Boruff lives in East Tennessee with her husband, three children, and an ever growing number of cats. She loves reading, watching TV, and procrastinating by browsing Facebook. L.A.'s passions include vampires, food, and listening to heavy metal music. She once won a Harry Potter trivia contest based on the books and lost one based on the movies. She has two bands on her bucket list that she still hasn't seen: AC/DC and Alice Cooper. Feel free to send tickets.

Printed in the USA
CPSIA information can be obtained
at www.ICGtesting.com
CBHW020346260824
13582CB00053B/1201

9 798869 323354